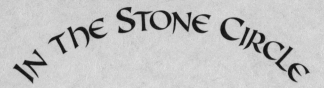

IN THE STONE CIRCLE

IN THE STONE CIRCLE

ELIZABETH CODY KIMMEL

SCHOLASTIC INC.

New York Toronto London Auckland Sydney
Mexico City New Delhi Hong Kong

ISBN 0-439-06259-4

12 11 10 9 8 7 6 5   1 2 3/0

Printed in the U.S.A.   40

First Scholastic Trade paperback printing, December 1998

Book design by Kristina Iulo

In memory of my dear father,
William Frederic Cody

In the Stone Circle

1

My life could not, under any circumstances, be worse. I'll admit, I've said this before. I said it when we moved to Ohio. I said it when my best friend, Charlotte Hawthorne, stopped speaking to me for a whole week for no reason at all. And I said it when my father accepted a job teaching medieval studies at this podunk college. That time I really meant it. I'm not saying I expected my father to be the Secretary of Defense, or a world-class sumo wrestler. I would have settled for less. But to be a professor of a subject so dead, so mind numbing it makes calculus look like a trip to Graceland . . . that is a heavy load to dump on anyone. Since I'm only fourteen, I don't have a life of my own. I rely completely on my dad, and since he has no life whatsoever, my chances are pretty much blown.

And, just when we've settled into our second

spectacularly dull year of Dad teaching in Mather, Ohio, things get worse. The medieval studies department lets Dad know it's time to start bucking for tenure. That's a phrase I'd never even heard until we got to Ohio, and now it's all the medieval-professor types can talk about. They're the worst department in the whole college. And why shouldn't they be? It's no coincidence that all of the grossest things that have ever happened took place in medieval times. When were all the really sick torture devices invented? Medieval times. When did the plague kill everyone in completely foul ways? Medieval times. When did everything smell totally disgusting? Medieval times. Even the word *medieval* sucks. Custom-made to trip you up in spelling bees and pop quizzes.

Tenure. There's another evil word. I'm not sure I totally grasp the concept, but I know if you're a college professor, you really want it, and if you get it, it's practically impossible to get fired from your job. To get it, though, you have to do all these really stupid things, like going to cocktail parties, and doing what my dad calls "currying favor," which is a smart person's way of saying "kissing butt." Another thing you pretty much have to do to get tenure is to get something published. Dad's magnum opus (he calls it his *magnopus*), hasn't exactly been written yet. Actually, it hasn't even been started yet. Dad really wants to be a tenured professor, and the medieval studies department made it pretty clear to him that he'd better get cracking on his book if he wanted to be in the running. All these things put together resulted in Dad's planning this horrible summer vacation: an expedition to a country sure to be so unexciting I may never completely recover. Guaranteed: no television, in-line skating, or shopping malls. I might as well start writing the essay now: *My Death-Defyingly Stupid Summer Vacation In —*

"Dad? Dad? What's the name of that place again?"

"Wales!"

Wales. Like, *wails.* Need I say more?

I stared glumly at my father over a generous helping of mashed potatoes.

"Just explain to me," I said, "just one more time, why you have to do this. And assuming you do, why I have to go with you."

My father sighed, and pushed some lima beans in hopeless little circles around his plate.

"Cristyn, don't make me go through this again," he said, continuing before I had a chance to comply. "You know how important it is that I write this book. In order to write about Wales, I need to *be* in Wales. Away from all of this. And I've got to have complete access to the materials in their libraries. It's only for two months."

"Couldn't you possibly reconsider writing your *magnopus* on, say, Puerto Rico? Tortola, maybe? Something interesting must have gone on in medieval Bermuda. Can't you write about that, Professor Stone?"

I turned my attention back to my mashed potatoes to avoid the look he was giving me.

"I thought multicultural was in this year," I muttered, softly enough so he couldn't quite hear me.

"Why are you so horrified by the idea of going to Wales, anyway?" he asked. "It's in your blood, after all."

"What do you mean, it's in my blood?" I asked.

"I mean it's in your blood. Your mother came from a Welsh family."

"She was American," I said, confused.

"Yes she was, but she was born in Gwynedd, where we're going. She lived there until she was ten. Haven't I told you this? Her mother and father were both Welsh. You have a Welsh name."

"I do not!" I said loudly, feeling unreasonably insulted.

"Cristyn is Welsh for Christine. I told you, kiddo, it's in your blood."

I was fairly certain he was making fun of me with the whole Welsh thing. I'd never heard anything about my mother's family being Welsh before, I was pretty sure of that. But then again, we rarely talked about my mother. I had practically no memory of her at all, except for two things. I knew she had flaming red hair, and I knew she loved to sing. Somehow, those things had stayed with me when the rest of the memories had faded. I was only three when she died, so I guess it kind of makes sense. Still, sometimes I feel guilty that I can't remember more about her. That I never ask.

"Anyway, I've told you that you'll have company," my father said with his mouth mostly full. "Erica's daughter, uh . . . whatever-her-name-is, is exactly your age. And her son is around eight. It's beautiful country over there. You guys will have a great time."

"Give me a break, Dad," I said. "We don't know anything about Erica's daughter what's-her-name. She could be a total cow. She could terrorize me for the entire summer. For that matter, we don't know anything about this Professor Erica, either. She could be a psychopath. She could put on a hockey mask and kill us all in our sleep." I watched Dad fight to hide a little smile.

"I've been swapping E-mail with Erica for over a year now," he said, "and never once has she mentioned a proclivity for wearing protective hockey equipment."

"You never know, Dad," I said, shaking my head solemnly. "You just never know."

"I told you, Charlotte," I said, shifting the phone to my left ear, "it's a done deal. Consider me gone."

"Cristyn," Charlotte said in her raspy, out-of-breath way, "I'm telling you he's on the verge of asking you out. If you leave now, it would only be the most totally devastating thing you could possibly do. This is your *life* we're talking about!"

"Shut up, Charlotte," I said. "You know my situation. The day after tomorrow, I'm leaving for Wales."

"Your life is, like, over," she repeated, snapping her gum.

"I am totally aware of that, Charlotte, but I really want to thank you for making sure I can't forget it."

"No problem," she replied. "So where is this place again? Canada?"

"Wales, Char," I said, rearranging myself on the couch so my feet stuck straight up in the air. "West of England. East of Ireland."

"Whatever," she said. "Do they get cable?"

"I don't even know if they have electricity," I replied, though I had it on good authority that they did.

"Sounds like someone's gonna have a rotten summer," Charlotte said.

"Look, Char, I've got to start packing, okay?"

"So what am I supposed to tell Geoff?" she asked, snapping her gum again.

"Tell him I hooked up with Owain Glyndwr."

"Who? Do I know him?" she asked, sounding excited for the first time in days.

"Joke, Char. Just a little joke. He's the guy my dad's writing about."

"And you're going out with him?"

I love Charlotte. I really do. But even Wales was starting to look refreshing compared to this conversation.

"Forget I said anything. I've got to pack. I'll call again before I go, okay?"

"Okay," she said. As usual, she hung up without saying good-bye. That's my Charlotte.

Actually, I was almost done packing, but a little lie to get Charlotte off the phone never hurt anybody. Dad had issued several warnings about the weather, so my suitcase was full of sweaters, boots, and foul-weather gear. And, of course, all the books I could cram into the suitcase. If there wasn't going to be television, at least I'd have one means of escape.

I packed one other thing, too. I didn't even know I was going to do it, until I had tossed it into my suitcase. Totally uncharacteristic. I packed a picture of my mother.

2

I was beginning to think I might actually die of exhaustion before ever reaching our destination. We'd flown into Manchester airport, staggered through customs, then dragged our belongings into a taxicab, which took us to the car rental agency the university wanted Dad to use. One thing I have to say about these British types is they have pretty cool cabs. Our cab was this enormous, shiny black thing, so clean it looked like we were the first humans ever to get into it. The backseat was as big as a decent-sized igloo, and even with all of our luggage piled at our feet, we still had room to stretch out our legs. The rental car, however, was another matter.

"Dad, I've seen mailboxes that are bigger than this car," I said nervously.

"Isn't it great?" he asked, heaving mightily at a suitcase in an attempt to wedge it into the trunk.

"That's what they drive over here. Little cars. The environment thanks you."

"Can't we get one of those taxi cars? Space is good, Dad. Isn't that what the American dream is all about?"

"Get in," he said, slamming the trunk closed. "Wales awaits us."

I climbed in and sat, petrified, in what should have been the driver's seat of the car.

"Just relax," said my father, climbing into the driver's seat and buckling his seat belt. "It's very simple. It's just the reverse of the American system. Driver's seat on the right side of the car. Traffic stays on the left side of the road. There's nothing to it."

"There's nothing to death by head-on collision, either. You mean to tell me they actually let you drive without lessons or anything? Don't they care about the safety of their own citizens?"

"Relax," my father repeated, shifting the car into first gear.

I braced myself, clutched my stomach protectively, and kept my eyes firmly shut as we pulled out of the car rental parking lot. I maintained this position for about five minutes, waiting to hear the shriek of brakes and the crunch of steel. When no accident happened, I relented and opened my eyes, cautiously scanning the road for oncoming vehicles.

"We should be there in about two hours," my father said, glancing at me.

"Don't look at me, Dad," I muttered, clenching and unclenching my fists. "Just watch the road, okay?"

He just grinned.

I don't know what I was expecting to see, but I was disappointed at the flat views of farms extending on either side of the road. My father gave a small cheer when we passed the WELCOME TO WALES sign, but it didn't look very exciting to me. Just lots of grass, and more sheep than I'd ever seen in my life. More sheep than I could possibly have imagined existed on the entire face of the planet. The ground looked like one massive, woolly wall-to-wall carpet. Dejected, I reached into the glove compartment and pulled out the rental agency magazine and studied the British driving rules. At least one of us was going to know how to keep legal on the motorway. I lost myself in an article about the strange world of British speed limits.

"Hey, Cris," my dad said after a while, and I looked up and caught my breath.

The ocean had come into view on our right side, and in the distance, looming up into the sky, were scores of huge, beautiful mountains that crashed down into the sea in a cascade of cliffs.

"Whoa," I said softly.

"That's Gwynedd," he said. "Mountains upon mountains. Mount Snowdon is there somewhere. It's the highest mountain in all of Wales. We can take a train all the way up to the top, if you want. On a clear day, you can see Scotland, I've heard."

I stared, amazed, at the mountains, some still covered with snow at the peak. Somewhere, in one of those valleys, my mother had been born. These mountains would have been a familiar sight to her. I closed my eyes, and still saw them looming up in front of me, and watched them in my mind's eye, transfixed, until the humming of the motor sang me to sleep. I slept, as they say, the sleep of the dead.

"Cristyn," I heard my father say as he shook my shoulder.

I opened my eyes. "Have we had a wreck?" I murmured.

"We're here. We're in Dolwyddelan," he said.

"Dollwithellen," I repeated sleepily.

"Come on. It's beautiful! Come see!"

They say a mother can muster up enough strength to lift a truck in order to save her child. Keeping this principle in mind, I willed my muscles to move, and they did. I got out of the car and stood in the driveway numbly, then turned after my father, who was already scrambling up the path.

The house stood at the end of a gravel walkway. It was a large, but not enormous, stone building, partially covered with ivy. The slate roof slanted steeply upward, flanked by a slender chimney on either side of the house. I stood, looking around at the sloping hills and stone fences, trying to identify the strange noises wafting up from the valley. It sounded like a lot of grumpy old men shouting one-syllable words at each other. Sheep, I thought. We're surrounded by sheep. Why do they sound so irritated? I quickly caught up with my father, who was standing in the driveway, staring at the house.

"My God," he murmured. "It can't be."

"What's wrong?" I asked, a little worried at his strange expression. "Dad? Is something wrong?"

He turned suddenly and looked at me strangely. "What?" he said.

"What is it?" I asked.

"Oh, it's nothing, Cris, I just . . . This house. It's the strangest thing. I think I've — your mother spent her last summer in Dolwyddelan in a rented house, before leaving for America. She had a little watercolor of it that she kept in our room."

"What?" I prompted. "And you think this is the same house?"

He shook his head. "I don't know. It looks so — I mean there are a lot of old stone houses in Dolwyddelan. No reason to think . . . But it doesn't matter. Let's get inside." He walked over to the heavy oak door, and fumbled with the keys. I didn't move for a moment. Fate is punishing us, I thought, for never talking about her.

"Anyway, it's beautiful, isn't it?" he asked with his back to me. "The real-estate lady said it was built in the sixteenth century, but that the foundations are hundreds of years older than that. Pretty amazing, huh? And it's ours for two months!"

Ours and the possibly psychopathic Erica's with her possibly degenerate children. I didn't voice that thought, though. My father looked distant and sad. I wanted to bring him back to me.

"It's fantastic, Dad. You can pick 'em."

"If only I could pick this lock," he said, struggling with the keys. "I can't make these work."

"Maybe there's another door around back," I said. "I'll go and check."

I left him muttering to himself and walked through a stone gateway onto a path that seemed to lead around the house. The grounds were lush and richly green, and the grass was soft beneath my feet. I allowed myself to experience a small moment of contentment. At least there would be plenty of scenic spots to steal away to, on the days it wasn't raining.

I rounded the back of the house and surveyed it. No door. I looked up at the arched windows on the second floor, wondering which room was mine. My eye was suddenly drawn back to the ground-floor window by a small movement, as if the curtain had been drawn slightly back. Keeping my eyes fixed on the spot, I walked directly to the window and peered inside. It was a kitchen. Cozy-looking, and no one there at all.

"Cristyn!" I heard my father shout from the front of the house. "I've done it! I'm in!"

I left the kitchen window and hurried to join my father inside the house.

I was having a strange dream, something involving a man galloping through mud on a horse, when my father awakened me.

"Cristyn? You've slept for three hours. It's almost seven o'clock at night."

I opened my eyes and stared at him, only vaguely recognizing who he was, and beyond caring.

"Erica and her kids just got in. Remember, Miranda's sharing this room with you. She's going to want to unpack. Honey? Are you awake?"

I managed a barely audible croak, but was unable to raise my head from the pillow. My father gave me a gentle pinch on the ear.

"Up and at 'em. Sleep any longer and you'll be up all night. Can you be downstairs in five?"

"Ten," I moaned, willing myself to die.

"Five," he said, moving toward the door. "For God's sake, Cris, you've got jet lag, not consumption."

I gave a little cough to cast some doubt over the issue, but he was already out the door. For an older guy, he was showing an annoying amount of pep. Reluctantly, I swung my feet onto the floor and stood up.

My room was pretty nice. There were large oak beams exposed on each wall, and the ceiling, also supported by the thick, dark beams, slanted sharply upward. There was a large window facing the grounds in the back of the house. Several acres of lawn ended abruptly in forest, and I could make out a little stone bridge at the very end of the property. Even more interesting was the little door by my bed that opened to reveal a spiral staircase, twisting sharply downward into what must be the kitchen below. That would be convenient for the occasional midnight snack, I thought. If only I wasn't stuck with a roommate.

I heard voices filtering up through the floorboards. Five minutes had just about passed, and it would be too embarrassing if Dad had to come up after me again. I took a quick look in the mirror, gasped in dismay at my puffy features, and walked through the main doorway and down the wide staircase that led to the front hall.

They were all gathered in the kitchen. I hesitated a bit at the door, wanting to check them out before they got a look at me, but my father dashed those hopes.

"Here she is! The dead have arisen. Cristyn, I'd like you to meet Erica Dunham; her son; Dennis; and her daughter, Miranda."

I mumbled hellos at them, and received two in return. Dennis was on his hands and knees examining the wood-burning stove, and he didn't bother to acknowledge me.

"Um, Dad? Do we have anything to drink?"

"Just water, I'm afraid," he replied, getting a glass down. "But it's good and cold."

He filled the glass and handed it to me, and I sat down at the kitchen table and took a long sip. I peered over the rim of the glass at Miranda while I drank. She was about my height, very slightly pudgy, with straight black hair. Her wire-rimmed glasses made her eyes look unnaturally large. She saw me watching her, and the corners of her mouth turned up slightly. It was kind of like looking at a baby, though — hard to tell if it was a smile, or just gas.

"Anyway, Derek," Mrs. Dunham was saying, "the real estate agent's directions were perfect. I had absolutely no trouble finding the place."

"A total lie," shouted Dennis, still lying on his stomach next to the stove. I caught Miranda's eye, and she nodded slightly, rolled her eyes, and looked away.

"Get off the floor, Dennis sweetheart," Mrs. Dunham said.

"No way," said Dennis, with his arm extended under the stove. "There's a whole bunch of really cool crud under here."

"He's eight," Mrs. Dunham said to my father with a little sigh.

"Nine's worse," my father replied with a grin.

I wasn't sure if I liked the look of Miranda's mother. She was slightly taller than her daughter, with none of Miranda's baby fat. Her dark hair was pulled back in a knot and held together with a little cloth twisty thing. She wore glasses, too, and they made her look a little severe. I made up my mind right away not to take any guff from her. I'd made it eleven years without a mother, and I wasn't going to start taking orders now.

"Cristyn?" my father was saying. "How about it? Can you show Miranda your room, and help get her settled in?"

"Sure," I responded, rising heavily to my feet. "Follow me."

We walked out of the kitchen and back up the staircase in silence. Miranda drew in her breath slightly as we walked into the bedroom.

"God, it's great!" she exclaimed. "You're probably bummed to have to share it with me."

"It's okay," I said untruthfully. "It will probably be fun, or whatever. So there's this big chest of drawers here, and that thing by the window is a wardrobe to hang things in. I haven't unpacked any of my stuff yet. I went straight to sleep when we got here."

"Seriously?" said Miranda. "I slept for five hours on the plane. I'm wired as hell. Where does this go?" she asked, pointing toward the little door. I opened it, and she stood next to me, peering down the dark staircase.

"It goes downstairs to the kitchen, I think," I told her. "It's like a secret passageway or something."

"Excellent," said Miranda, her eyes widening. "We can, like, escape. If necessary."

Something about the idea of escaping excited me, in spite of its impracticalities.

"Exactly," I said.

Miranda walked over to her bed and plopped down onto it with a heavy sigh.

"So is this trip as much of a nightmare for you as it is for me?" she asked, reclining.

"Basically," I replied. "This guy I like was supposedly getting ready to ask me out after, like, nine weeks of totally ignoring me."

"My friend Jeanette's parents agreed to chaperon a trip for a bunch of us to San Francisco," Miranda said. "Of course, it was totally out of the question for me. My mother is fixated on ruining my life. Like it's possible to even have a life in Indiana."

"Yeah," I said sympathetically. "I kind of feel the same way about Ohio."

"And Wales doesn't look like much of an improvement," she said. "I mean, what do they expect us to do for two months?"

"I have no idea," I said. "Dad bought these survey maps of the area, and he keeps showing them to me and pointing out these supposedly exciting places to walk to. I think he's planning for me to become some kind of junior hiker or something. He thinks it will be good for me to have some time away from the horrors of American culture. That's what he calls it. The horrors of American culture."

Miranda laughed. "I got the same line from my mother," she said. "A little fresh air will do you guys some good, she keeps saying. You'll be a better person for it. Like, do you know one person in the world who is a better person because of fresh air?"

"Can't think of one," I said. "Except Dad, maybe, if that counts."

"So your parents are divorced, too?" she asked.

"Not exactly," I said stupidly. "I mean, my mother's

dead. They were married, though, when she died."

Miranda sat up and looked at me carefully. "Really?" she asked. "Since when?"

"I was three," I replied.

"Did she . . . I mean . . ."

"She was thrown from a horse," I said. "Broke her neck."

"God," Miranda replied. "I'm really sorry."

"It's okay," I said. "I mean, I barely remember her."

"Is that her?" Miranda asked, pointing to the picture on my dresser.

"Yeah," I replied, then turned my attention to my suitcase. Funny, the picture was the only thing I'd unpacked.

We'd eaten dinner early, then each retired to our rooms. Miranda had kept the light on to read a while, but it didn't prevent me from falling immediately into a deep sleep. What seemed like hours later, I suddenly awoke. I wasn't sure if I had heard a noise, or if I had simply awakened out of body-clock confusion. I lay staring at the ceiling for a minute, then I heard the noise again. It was a soft, rustling noise. Clutching the covers protectively up to my chin, I looked around the room as my eyes adjusted to the dark. There was a dark shape by the window. Had Miranda hung her coat up on a hook there or something? Then the shadow moved, and my heart began to beat wildly. Somebody, or something, was standing over Miranda's bed. I stared in horror, unable to look away. The figure reached out toward Miranda's head, and I heard the sound of something liquid being poured onto her pillow. Miranda shrieked, leaped out of the bed, and lunged at the shadowy figure.

"Dennis, you putrid little scuz!" she shrieked, wrestling the figure to the floor. I sat up and switched on the light, watching in amazement as Miranda, her hair partially soaked, pummeled her little brother.

"Ow! Ow!" he cried. "Get off me, lard butt!"

Miranda responded to that by administering a smack on his head. Dennis uttered another shriek, then wriggled free of her grasp and shot out of the room.

"The little brat!" she muttered, wringing out her hair. "I swear, Cristyn, I tried everything to lose him in the airport, but he just kept turning up, like Hansel and Gretel with a homing beacon or something."

"Does he behave this way often?" I asked, watching her climb back into bed.

"He is a creature of the devil. A total nightmare.

And if we're not very careful, he will make our lives a living hell."

"Then I guess we'd better be careful," I replied, switching the light off again. If Charlotte could see me now, I thought, then I drifted back into blessed sleep.

3

By the time Miranda and I came down for breakfast the next morning, my father had already driven into town for groceries. The kitchen was freezing. In fact, the whole house was freezing. I could actually see my breath. Dennis was sitting at the kitchen table chewing on a muffin. He stuck out his tongue at Miranda, and she glared back at him.

"Good morning, girls!" said Mrs. Dunham brightly. "Did you sleep well?"

"Fine," said Miranda, kicking me gently under the table. I was surprised, but if Miranda chose not to rat out her little brother, who was I to argue?

"Mr. Stone's gone into the village to stock up on groceries," Mrs. Dunham said. "I'm afraid that all we have for breakfast in the meantime is English muffins."

"That's fine," said Miranda.

"If you like, you can have a muffin now and when Derek brings — "

"A muffin is fine, Mother," repeated Miranda, sounding irritated.

Mrs. Dunham appeared not to notice her daughter's tone as she placed two muffins into the oven to brown. Dennis took a particularly large bite of his muffin, chewed it several times, then opened his mouth to display its contents with pride. A soggy lump of muffin tumbled off his tongue and fell onto the table with a light thud. Miranda made a disgusted noise and jumped up from the table.

"Forget it — I'm not hungry!" she said. "I'm going outside."

I was hungry, but I didn't want to be left alone with Mrs. Dunham and the See-Food Monster, so I muttered something about not being hungry either, and followed Miranda out the front door. She was heading through the stone gate to the path I'd walked on when Dad and I first arrived. I had to run a little to catch up with her.

"The two of them make me crazy," she said without turning to look at me. "She nags and he bugs. They're a matching set."

I couldn't think of anything to say. I didn't have any siblings, and my father and I were pretty tight.

Seeing Miranda coping with her family made me suddenly thankful for my own situation, even if it did land me in Wales for the summer.

We rounded the back of the house, and paused on the lawn, surveying our surroundings.

"There's a stone bridge down there by the tree line," I said. "You can see it from our window."

"Let's check it out," said Miranda, and we set off across the grass. The cloud cover was burning off, and the sun was beginning to shine warmly through. I shivered a little, and turned my face up to its warmth. It looked as though our first full day in Wales might actually be a sunny one. The stone bridge came into view, and now I could see that it spanned a narrow but deep-looking stream with a sandy, rocky bed. We walked onto the bridge and leaned over the side, staring at the stream.

"This bridge is old," said Miranda.

"Do you think?" I asked.

"It's at least as old as the house. Look at it, it's made of the same kind of stone. It's probably been here for four hundred years."

I digested that information for a moment, imagining travelers of centuries past standing where Miranda and I stood now. A little shiver ran up my spine at the thought.

"Let's see where this path goes," said Miranda, already walking off the bridge. I followed her into the woods, where the air was several degrees cooler. The path was worn clean of grass, but as we walked deeper into the forest it grew more narrow and less distinct. I was about to suggest that we turn back, when we came to a small clearing. In the center of the clearing was a slightly raised, grassy area surrounded by a circle of large rocks.

"A campfire circle," I said excitedly, imagining Miranda and I stealing away to toast marshmallows and tell ghost stories.

"It doesn't look as if anyone's built a fire in here for a long time," commented Miranda, seating herself on one of the rocks.

"It's beautiful, though," I said, walking to the center of the circle, and Miranda nodded in agreement. I lay down on my back in the damp grass and stared up at the sky. Something about the puffy cotton-shaped clouds brought a memory of my mother to the surface, and though I could not place the scene, I felt that we had spent such a morning together, lying in the grass and watching the sky. Her hair hung down below her shoulders, I thought, and it was as bright as a sunset. I breathed deeply, letting the image linger, until something sharp struck me on the forehead. I let out a little shriek and sat up.

"What?" asked Miranda, looking slightly aggravated.

"Something hit me on the head," I said, rubbing the sore spot ruefully.

"What, like an acorn?" she asked.

"But there aren't any trees overhead," I replied.

"Then what — " She stopped as another small object flew through the air, narrowly missing her head. She turned to survey the woods with a keen eye, and I sensed some motion there.

"Dennis, you are DEAD!" she shrieked, jumping to her feet.

I heard Dennis howling with laughter as he tore back up the path toward the house. Miranda ran a few steps after him, and then stopped.

"Fink," she muttered. "Loathsome. Little. Toad," she added, emphasizing each word.

"He was just trying to get our attention," I said. "He's probably just bored or something."

"Wrong," Miranda said, pulling her features into a scowl. "He's devoting his life to irritating me. Sometimes I just don't think I can take it for another minute. He's been this way since the divorce, which was over a year ago, and Mother couldn't care less. I don't even tell on him anymore, because every time I do she gives me a lecture. Me! She tells me how difficult this past year has been on him, and how unfeeling I'm being. One time, he put mayonnaise in my pillowcase, and she told me to stop be-

ing so hard on him. Hard on *him*!! It's just so unfair, Cristyn, you wouldn't believe it!"

"Sorry," I said. "I'm an only child. I've never
really had to deal with this stuff."

"You're lucky," she said, still scowling a little.

"Think of it this way," I said. "For the summer, at
least, he's outnumbered. We're more than a match
for him."

"That's right," she said. "We're more than a
match for the little twerp."

She brightened visibly and straightened up.

"Okay," she said. "Now I'm hungry. Want to go
back?"

I nodded, and we headed back onto the path
through the woods. As we crossed the stone bridge,
she took my arm in hers, and that made me smile.

"Will that work?" I said to my father, who was
carefully unpacking his laptop computer. "Isn't the
electricity different here, or something?"

"Something," he replied, rummaging in a box
that had just been delivered. "But I come prepared.
Electrical adapter," he said, pulling it out of the box
and waving it triumphantly. "Plus a spare, plus a car-
ton of batteries. And, in the highly unlikely event of
total meltdown, there's an old typewriter in the
kitchen."

"You on a typewriter? That's something I'd like to see," I said, smiling. Even on a computer with spell-check, Dad's typos were legendary.

"I'll do just fine, thank you. Anyway, it won't be necessary. Erica's got a computer, too, so we'll always have backup."

"Are you guys writing this book together?" I asked, pulling some books out of the box.

"Oh, no," my father replied, wiping a dusty hand across his face. "Erica's work will have a much broader spectrum, whereas I'm concentrating solely on the fifteenth century and Owain Glyndwr."

"My hot date," I murmured, thinking mournfully of Charlotte.

"What?" my father asked.

"Nothing. Where do you want these?" I asked, brandishing a two-volume set of medieval history books.

"I'll take them. I want those right here by the desk. What's this?"

I followed his gaze to the desk and saw immediately what he was looking at. It was a picture of my mother. It was my picture — the one from my room.

"Umm, it's mine," I said, coloring slightly.

"Okay," he said, looking carefully at me. "I'm certainly glad to keep it here if that's what — "

"No," I said, grabbing the picture. "I mean, it's my picture, but I left it upstairs in my room. Dennis must have taken it and put it here. He is totally rude."

"Okay," my father said slowly.

"I'm sorry, Dad," I said, holding the picture against my sweater.

"Sorry? Oh, honey, no, don't be sorry. I'm glad you brought the picture. I think that's good. I mean, do you think about her a lot?"

I didn't know what to say to that. We just never talked about her. I didn't know how the idea of her made him feel. I didn't want him to be any sadder than he usually was.

"No," I said quickly. "I mean, you know. Every once in a while, or whatever. I don't know. That was a really long time ago, Dad."

"Yes," he said softly.

"So anyway," I said, feeling really uncomfortable, "I guess I'll go upstairs and put this back."

"Okay, honey," he said, looking distant. "Thanks for helping."

"No problem," I said as I left.

The stairs creaked as I climbed up them. The smell of ancient wood was becoming familiar to me. There was something of an actual home in this place that appealed to me. Miranda had real possibilities, too, and it was a nice change of pace. Maybe, I thought as I reached the top step, this summer won't be so bad after all.

I came to a stop as I walked into our bedroom. All of the furniture had been pushed into the middle of the room.

That Dennis, I thought, furious. Someone is going to have to kill him. And it had better be soon.

4

Over the next few days, Dad and Mrs. Dunham settled into a routine of studying, driving off to the local library, and returning with piles of dusty books and papers. They gave us some brief instructions on creating some kind of "walking regimen," but we were left pretty much on our own. Miranda and I explored the grounds more thoroughly, and Dennis did his best to tag along, teasing and running about crazily, until Miranda finally managed to discourage him. I thought he was sort of cute, actually, and kind of enjoyed watching him tear all over the place, but Miranda was clearly not charmed.

"We're better off without him," she said when he finally trudged off alone, hanging his head. "He's a royal pain in the butt."

We came to the end of a path that had started from the front of the house and led up a good-sized hill. Miranda leaned on a stone fence, breathing heavily and pushing the hair from her face.

"Have you ever," she moaned between breaths, "seen so many sheep in your life? What do they do with all of them? What possible purpose could they serve?"

"Wool, I guess," I said, staring at the fuzzy masses in wonder.

"What do they do all day?" she asked. "Imagine being a sheep. Look at them. They have two activities. Eating and sleeping."

"And standing," I added, laughing. "A lot of them are just standing around."

"Why?" she cried, sounding exasperated. "What does it mean? Think about it, Cristyn. I mean, what are they actually doing? Thinking? What could a sheep stand around thinking about all day long?"

"Sweaters?" I asked, and she laughed.

"Yeah, maybe they're thinking, What am I doing this for? To be a pullover? To be a pale pink button-down? Why couldn't I have been a cow? Then I at least could have been something leather, something rock-and-roll radical."

"But to be leather, they'd have to kill you," I pointed out. "At least if you're a sheep, they just take your wool and leave you alone."

"To grow more sweaters. To clothe the freezing masses. Life is just one big haircut to them."

"They're staring at us," I said, slightly alarmed. "Like they blame us, or something."

"It's not my fault!" Miranda shouted at them. "This sweater is one hundred percent cotton!"

I laughed, and a couple of sheep bleated in response.

"So you and your dad seem, like, tight, or whatever," she said, and I nodded.

"Yeah, you could say that," I replied, zipping up my jacket as the wind picked up. "He's a good guy."

"Mine, too," she said, staring off at the sheep. "Not that she ever lets me see him. But my dad is definitely cool. Much cooler than her."

There was a story there that I didn't think I wanted to hear, so I didn't say anything.

"So do you, you know . . ."

"Do I what?" I asked.

"You know. Do you, like, miss her?"

"My mother?" I asked, surprised.

"Yeah," she said, toying with her glasses.

"I don't know," I said. "I mean, there's nothing to miss. I was three, you know. We didn't exactly have this meaningful relationship or anything."

"Don't you remember her at all?" she asked.

"I don't know. I guess. I mean, there are little things, like her red hair and stuff. Her hands. I have this real clear memory of her buttoning up my winter coat all the way to the top, and her hands smelling really soapy and clean." Actually, I hadn't remembered that until that very moment, as if just talking about her was enough to release the memory.

"God, that's so sad," Miranda said.

"No it isn't," I replied quickly. "It's no great tragedy or anything. I barely even think about her at all."

"So why'd you bring her picture?" she pressed, and I scowled slightly.

"No reason," I said. "So, Miranda, tell me something. What, exactly, are we going to do for the next two months?"

She sighed. "Eat. Sleep. Stand around staring."

"Thinking about sweaters!" I cried, and she let out a little shriek.

"We're doomed," she howled, startling the sheep.

"Let's race," I called, already thundering down the path.

I won.

5

During dinner, Mrs. Dunham and my father got totally into this conversation about Edward the First, or somebody. I mean, they were completely oblivious to the world — it was that kind of thing. We could have set the table on fire and they probably wouldn't have noticed until the whole house had gone up in flames.

Miranda caught her little brother's eye and mouthed "You are dead," but Dennis just grinned.

"Hey, Cristyn," he said. "Lookit. Cristyn! Hey!"

"What?" I said, trying to sound exasperated.

"I can burble a pea. Wanna see? Cristyn, wanna see?"

"Burble?" I asked.

"Ignore him," muttered Miranda.

"Yeah, I can burble a pea, look!" Dennis picked up a pea from his plate, leaned his head all the way back, and placed the pea on his lips. Then he took a deep breath through his nose, and blew out gently through his mouth. The pea lifted and gently floated about a half inch above his lips. Delighted, I laughed out loud.

"Wasn't that cool?" Dennis shouted, snapping his head forward so the pea shot onto the table. "Did you like it?"

"It's the most stupid thing I've ever seen," snapped Miranda. "He does it every damn time we have peas."

"Cristyn, did you like it? Did you?"

I nodded at him, sort of hoping Miranda wouldn't catch it. Dennis beamed at me.

"Like what?" I heard my father say.

"I burbled a pea," said Dennis, still grinning. "Cristyn liked it."

"Burbled?" said my father.

"Is it true your mother is dead?" Dennis asked, totally out of the blue.

The table fell completely silent. No one looked at Dennis. No one looked at anyone, actually.

"Dennis," hissed Miranda, breaking the silence, "you are the most stupid, most retarded, most lamebrained geek ever to walk the face of the earth."

"What?" asked Dennis, his eyes growing larger.

"You are so totally moronic," continued Miranda, "that you have no concept of the fact that you just said the most horrible, most rude thing that's ever come out of your mouth in the eight hideous years you've been alive. You completely wigged out Cristyn. She'll probably never forgive you, and neither will I."

I don't know what surprised me more: the fact that Miranda was being so awful to her brother, the fact that Mrs. Dunham did absolutely nothing to stop it, or the fact that cocky Dennis was beginning to whimper, and his lower lip was beginning to tremble as he fought back the tears.

"I di — I didn't mean . . ." he faltered.

"It's cool, Dennis," I said quickly. "It's no big deal. Yes, my mom is dead. She died a really really long time ago, so it's okay to talk about it. I'm not wigging out. Honest. How about burbling another pea for my dad?"

Dennis's lower lip stopped trembling, replaced by another grin. He tilted his head back and commenced burbling. As my father began to laugh, Miranda shook her head and stood up.

"I'm finished," she said coldly. "So if no one minds, I'm out of here."

No one said anything, so Miranda plunked her plate in the sink and flounced out of the room. She was obviously irritated at me, and I didn't like it one bit. Over pea burbling? Was the girl crazy?

"Edward the First," said Mrs. Dunham very matter-of-factly, "was a despot."

The Dunhams are really very strange.

"Will you please just say something to me?" I asked.

Miranda didn't look up from her book.

"Miranda? What is your problem? Is this about Dennis?"

Miranda slammed her book shut and glared at me.

"My whole life," she said, "is about people being nice to Dennis. My mother worries that she isn't being nice enough to Dennis. She tells me *I'm* not being nice enough to Dennis. His teacher calls from school to let us know that everyone is being really nice to Dennis, because they know how hard the divorce was for him. Dennis Dennis Dennis! It's like I don't exist! And as if that isn't bad enough, I make a new friend and the first time I turn around, she's coddling my little brother. To hell with that! I don't need either of you!"

"Coddling? What exactly is your definition of coddling? I don't recall signing any document that stated that speaking to Dennis was an act of war. You're blowing this way out of proportion. It's no big deal."

"It is a big deal. You said we'd be more than a match for him. You said — I thought you understood, Cristyn. I thought . . . just forget about it, okay? Just forget everything. Why don't you go downstairs and play Go Fish with him or something. You'd probably like that."

I didn't know what to do, so I just stood there. She was behaving like a child, and I was mad, but I really didn't want us to have a falling out when things had started so well. It was going to be a long summer. I needed her. And besides, I really hadn't meant to hurt her feelings.

"Miranda . . ." I began.

"I said just — "

Neither of us saw where it came from. We only saw it falling down in a straight line — a small, shiny object. It was as if it had materialized out of thin air. It hit the floor, and rolled under Miranda's bed.

"Did you see that?" I gasped.

"What was it?" Miranda asked, climbing out of her bed.

"It's under here," I said, crouching by her bed.

"Do you see it? Do you have it?" Miranda asked.

"Not yet," I said, lying flat on my stomach and feeling around the floor under the bed. "Did you see it fall? Where did it come from?"

"The twerp, of course," said Miranda. "He was

41

listening at the door. Threw it at us. Aiming for my head, probably, but he's a lousy shot."

"The door was shut," I said softly, and Miranda took note of that fact and fell silent. Reaching, my hand finally connected with the object. I grasped it and pulled it toward me. Miranda leaned over me as I sat up, extended my hand, and opened my palm. A worn, shiny, circular object glittered faintly in my hand.

"A coin," said Miranda, reaching for it, but I drew my hand slightly away and held it to my face.

"I can't see anything on it," I said, examining it. "Whatever was on the face has been worn away. It looks really old, though."

"Let me see," she said, snatching it from me. "Can't make anything out. You're right, though, it is a coin. It looks like there was a face, or a head of somebody on this side." She turned it over and examined the other side.

"Wait, look at this!" she said. I leaned in close to get a better look.

"One . . . two . . . uh . . . nine? No, eight . . . and . . . two. Twelve eighty-two. God," I said, sitting back on my heels. "Do you think that's the year it was made?"

"The coin wasn't minted this way," said Miranda matter-of-factly. "Look how sloppy the numbers are. Someone scratched this on by hand with something sharp."

"Why?"

"Dennis probably did it. Another brain-dead prank."

"Dennis didn't do this, and you know it," I said. "You saw it. The coin fell straight down, not in an arc. It came from up there." I pointed at the ceiling.

Miranda digested this information and ran her hands through her hair nervously. She didn't speak.

"Miranda?" I prompted.

"What do you want me to say? Things don't just fall out of thin air."

I took the coin and held it up to the light.

"They do now," I said.

Miranda stared at the coin, then gave a small nod.

"So what do you think?" I asked.

"I think," she said, removing her glasses, "that we're going to sleep with the lights on tonight."

And we did.

6

"There are mice in this house," announced Miranda at breakfast the next morning.

"There are not," said Mrs. Dunham, looking shocked.

"There are," said Miranda. "I heard them scratching last night."

"I heard them, too," I said truthfully. In fact, I had already proposed to Miranda that the scratching sounds had not been mice, but were, in fact, somehow related to the dropping coin. Apparently she found my idea entirely too disturbing, and was stubbornly sticking to the mouse theory in spite of my arguments. Plucking a souvenir out of thin air was one thing, but scratching spirits were, for Miranda, not within the realm of acceptability.

"Cool!" shouted Dennis. "Can we catch them? Can we eat them?"

"I really hate mice," Mrs. Dunham said weakly. "Derek, can you take care of them?"

"Oh, come on, Erica," said my father, slathering jam onto a muffin. "This house is over four hundred years old. You've got to expect a mouse or two."

"I would appreciate it, Derek," she said firmly, "if you could get some traps from town."

"As you like," my father said, shrugging. "What are you kids going to do today? Did you look at the Ordnance Survey map I gave you? If you go down the driveway and cross the road, there's a little pond in a clearing. We could make you up a little picnic. You could go swimming."

"Dad, take a look out there," I said, ruefully watching the rain stream down in sheets against the window. "No point in even thinking about going outside."

"Oops, sorry," he said, giving me a sheepish grin.

"I swear, Dad, you are the original absentminded professor."

"What was your name again?" he asked, and I rolled my eyes at the joke.

"I've got to run into town to exchange these books at the university library," said Mrs. Dunham. "Maybe you guys could come along and pick out some books."

"Um, Erica, I don't think they have a young people's section there," said my father.

"It's okay, Dad," I said. "I brought piles of books. Look, we'll figure something out. Maybe the weather will clear later, and we can check out the pond then."

"Now I want you girls to include Dennis in your plans," said Mrs. Dunham. Miranda muttered something under her breath.

"Miranda," said Mrs. Dunham, "we have discussed this."

"Whatever," she said, getting up. "I have to go make my bed."

She walked out of the kitchen as her mother looked after her.

I got up and took the rest of the plates to the sink.

"I can do these," I said to Mrs. Dunham, who had started washing the dishes.

"That's all right, dear," she said, scrubbing a plate violently. "I'll do them. Run along now."

Run along now? I shook my head slightly and turned back to the table. My father had left, and Dennis was investigating a small door by the wood-burning stove. It was obviously the door that led to our bedroom stairs, but I didn't feel like getting into an exchange with him, so I went into the study after my father. He smiled at me as I walked in.

"Miranda's *weird*, Dad," I said softly. "She's moody. She throws fits. She has definite lunatic potential. And her mother has kind of a weird thing going, too." He got up and shut the study door, then turned back to me.

"They're okay, Cris. I mean, things are definitely out of whack with the whole family right now, but they're not weird. Not that weird, anyway," he added, with a little smile. "They've all had a rough time of it."

"What do you mean?" I asked.

"Well, I really shouldn't talk about it."

"Give me a break, Dad," I said.

"Just don't say anything, then. Erica and her husband's divorce became final about a year ago. She got custody of the children, and he had weekend visitation rights. She told me that one day, after a Little League game where he was meeting Dennis, there was some kind of a problem. And shortly after that, he just took off. Skipped town. No phone calls, no letters, no visits, nothing, for six months. Apparently, he got back in touch with Erica briefly in the spring, and arranged to come up for Miranda's birthday. But something came up, I guess, and he never showed up. That was three months ago, and he hasn't contacted them since. He's been having Erica's university forward his checks to her."

"Oh," I said. "I guess she has a right to be weird, then."

"I guess," my father said. "Anyway, I think

maybe Dennis somehow got it into his head that it was his fault that his father left. He had been begging him to come to a Little League game, and he finally got his dad to agree, and that was the day he left for good. I guess Dennis figured his father got mad at him and left."

"What a rotten father," I said.

"Apparently. Anyway, things have been pretty tense for the Dunhams since then. Everybody's mad at everybody else. So just tread carefully, okay?"

"It's really hard, Dad," I said. "Sometimes I just want to take Miranda's head off. Things started out okay, and she can be good company, and everything, but she has this thing about her brother. If I even look at him, she gets all mad like I've attacked her or something."

"I know, honey," he said. "You know, I really think that if you can keep a lid on this thing, and try to keep it from becoming a war between the two of you, it could be really good for everyone. Maybe Miranda will loosen up with Dennis. I know she's a little explosive right now, but do you think you might be able to hang in there? I really think things will start to improve if you do."

"Okay," I said. "If that's what you want. And to be honest, I don't exactly want to alienate the only friend I have in this country. Except for you, that is."

"Good girl," he said, smiling at me. "I'm sorry, you know, that I didn't think more about you guys when I planned this trip. I should have had more stuff for you to do. I should have done a little research to see what's around."

"We'll be all right, Dad," I said. "In a twisted kind of a way, you're probably right that we should be away from television, and the mall, and everything. I've always wondered what Laura Ingalls Wilder did all day, and I guess I'm about to find out."

"You're a princess," he said, giving me a big smile.

"Of course I am," I replied. "So how's the *magnopus*?"

"Just a pile of notes at the moment," he said, turning toward the desk. "I've almost — oh."

My mother's picture was back on his desk.

"My mother's picture was back on Dad's desk again," I said to Miranda.

"Dennis must die," she said, her eyes gleaming.

"But I'm beginning to wonder if it was Dennis," I said. "After the coin, and the scratching . . ."

"Mice," she said quickly.

"Say what you want," I said. "But it didn't sound like mice to me. Think about it. The coin appearing, the noises, stuff moving around. I think it's all the same thing."

"Why would a . . ."

"Ghost," I prompted.

"Whatever — why would it be so interested in your mother's picture?"

"Why would Dennis?" I asked.

"It would take a rocket scientist to figure out what goes on in that boy's head."

"Then let's ask him," I said.

"He lies," she replied.

"We can try. And who knows, maybe the ghost is doing stuff around him, too. Maybe — "

"Stop right there," she said. "We can ask him about the picture, but we can't tell him why. I don't want him reporting to Mom that we've been scaring him. Believe me, I'll get in major trouble."

"All right, then," I said. "So let's ask him."

We walked out of the room together, and down the hall to Dennis's room, but he was not inside. He'd been retreating to the study more frequently, as it became obvious that he wasn't welcome with us. He was probably there now, and Miranda certainly was not willing to ask him about the picture in front of our parents.

"Let's do something else," said Miranda.

"We could explore the secret staircase," I suggested, and Miranda's eyes widened.

"Excellent," she said. "I even have a flashlight somewhere. Maybe we can find old messages on the wall or something."

She began rummaging through her drawers for the flashlight.

"Wouldn't the messages be in Welsh?" I asked.

Miranda just shrugged and continued sifting through her clothes.

"Here it is," she said. "Shall we explore?"

"Let's do it."

We opened the doorway, and Miranda shined the flashlight down. The staircase was extremely narrow, and it curled down in a tight spiral.

"Okay," she said, handing me the flashlight. "You go first."

I took the flashlight from her and stepped onto the staircase. The doorway was low, and I had to stoop to get inside.

"Be careful," I said, taking a few cautious steps. "The stairs are really narrow. They must have had really tiny feet in the sixteenth century."

"They must have been short, too," said Miranda from behind me.

We progressed about halfway down the staircase, and then I paused to examine the wall. I couldn't make out any writing. All I could see was the rough, dark surface of stone.

"Keep going," said Miranda, and I continued down the stairs.

"Here it is," I said.

"Here what is?"

"The door to the kitchen."

"Let me see." She stood beside me on the small, dark landing as I illuminated the kitchen door with the light.

I paused for a moment, then shined the flashlight around.

"Look at this," I said, pointing the flashlight downward. "The staircase doesn't stop here. It keeps going down!"

"Then so do we," said Miranda.

"But there's nothing down there, is there? There's no cellar in this house, is there?"

I felt Miranda's hand planted on my back.

"Only one way to find out," she said, pushing me gently. "Go, girl, go."

So I went.

We descended what seemed like another half level or so, until the light of my flashlight found a large square of oak ahead of us.

"A door," I said.

There was enough room for two to stand side by side there, and Miranda came and stood beside me.

We stared at the door. There was a rusty iron dead bolt near the top of the door.

"We'll never get that open," I said. "It looks like it hasn't been touched in years."

"We can try," said Miranda, and she reached up and grasped the bolt with both hands. She strained for several moments, but the lock didn't budge.

"Ugh," she said, rubbing her hands. "You try."

I put both hands on the lock and pulled with all my strength. The bolt slid open with much less resistance than I'd expected.

"Are you ready?" I asked.

Miranda nodded, and I pulled the door toward me. It swung open with a slight squeak. We both hesitated. Through the door, we could see that the stairs continued down. It felt very cold and damp. There was a heavy, musty smell in the air. And it was very, very dark.

"So," I said.

"So," Miranda replied, her voice a little shaky.

"Do you want to, um, save this for another time or something?"

"That would be totally lame," she replied, and slipping her arm through mine, she maneuvered us both through the door, and down the first several steps.

The drop in temperature was severe. It must have been ten degrees colder than it had been on the other side of the door. We descended a total of three or four steps, then hesitated.

"Shine the light down there," commanded Miranda, and I did so. "Can you see anything?"

"Just black," I said. "Look, I'm not a wimp, or anything, but I don't exactly like this. We need a bigger light or something."

"I agree," said Miranda, to my relief. "Let's — "

I never heard the rest of her sentence. It was eclipsed by the sound of the oak door slamming shut behind us. Seconds later, we heard the unmistakable sound of the dead bolt sliding back into place.

7

My fists ached from hammering on the door, and my voice was growing hoarse from shouting.

"Nobody hears us, Miranda," I said. "It's no good."

"How could the door just shut like that?" she cried. "How could it lock? It must have been Dennis."

"Dennis couldn't reach high enough to lock it, Miranda. I think . . . I mean, I don't think the door shut by itself."

"Oh, my God," she moaned. "Please don't tell me we've been locked in the cellar by that — whatever-it-is. What does it want?"

"I don't know," I said softly.

"Mother," Miranda howled, banging on the door. "Get us out of here!"

"I don't think they're going to hear us in the

study," I said. "Not with that Gregorian chanting thing they play on the stereo."

"What I would really, really like to know," said Miranda after a moment, "is how you could drop the flashlight like that."

"I told you," I said. "You knocked it out of my hands when the door slammed."

"I never touched you!" she protested.

"Well I'm sorry, Miranda, but you did. You jumped, and your arm or something hit my hand and the flashlight went down the stairs. It must have broken on the way down."

"I did not," she repeated, "touch you."

"Did," I replied.

"Did not," she said.

"Miranda, it so totally doesn't matter anymore, okay? I don't care that you did it. I'm not, like, mad or anything. I'm just explaining to you how it happened."

"Cristyn," she said firmly, "you're not getting it. Listen to me. I — did — not — touch — you."

The realization of what that meant hit us at the same time. Something had touched me. If it wasn't Miranda, then whatever had been making noises and moving things around was on the stairs with us. Now.

"We're going to die," Miranda whispered.

"No we're not," I said emphatically. "I am not going to die. I have no intention of just skipping off the planet and leaving everyone behind like some people."

"What are you talking about?" she asked, and I started to say I didn't know. But I did know.

"You have no idea," I said after a moment, "what it's like to love someone and hate them at the same time."

"What someone?" she asked.

Maybe it was the darkness. Maybe I really did think something lurking in the blackness was about to do us in. Things just started coming out of my mouth that I barely knew I'd been thinking.

"I . . . God, I've never said this out loud before. My mother. I feel that way about my mother. I mean, I love her because she's my mother. And the little bit that I do remember about her is good. I think, you know, that I really did love her a lot when she was alive. But she left me. Sometimes I really hate her for it. There's this big space in my life where she's supposed to be, and nobody can fill it."

"I thought you said it didn't bother you."

"Well maybe it does, okay? My dad almost never talks about her, so there's all this stuff about her that I don't even know, and I'm too afraid to ask. I mean, supposedly I'm half Welsh, and I never knew that. Can you imagine not knowing something like that about yourself? And it'd be one thing if he had married somebody else or something, and felt weird talking about her, but there's nobody! He doesn't even go out on dates! Nothing! And I can't hate him for it, because that would be totally harsh when he's been through so much. So then I hate her."

"But it wasn't her fault she died," came Miranda's voice from the darkness. "How can you hate her for something she had no control over?"

"How can you hate Dennis when he had no control over your dad skipping town?"

There was silence for a moment, and I thought I might have gone too far.

"I know," she said finally. "It doesn't make sense. But he's so awful, and he gets all the attention! No matter what I do, my mother only pays attention to him. You've seen what he's like."

"Was it always this way?" I asked.

"No," she said. "I mean, he was always a pest, but we used to get along, too. We had some good times. Before, you know."

"Yeah," I replied.

"He's just making it so hard on me, Cris. He hasn't done or said anything even remotely nice since Dad left. It's like, not my fault, you know? And he's taking it out on me, or something. All the stupid tricks he plays. The thing is, I could probably handle it if it was just him. But my mother has been this way for practically a year now. She totally fawns over Dennis, and the only time she ever talks to me is to criticize. It's like when Dad left the family, I got kicked out, too. Only I didn't want to leave."

"Yeah," I said again.

"Anyway," she said, "I'm sorry. I know I've been . . . well, I'm sorry. And I'm sorry about your mom."

"I'm sorry about your dad." She felt for my hand, and squeezed it.

"What was that?" she asked suddenly.

"What?" I said, my heart already racing.

"Listen," she whispered, putting the death grip on my hand.

I listened.

"The scratching," I said, feeling sick.

"Coming from down there," she said.

"Go away!" I shouted, and the scratching suddenly stopped.

"Good. Okay," said Miranda. "So we'll just shout every couple of minutes, which we have to do anyway, in case someone goes into the kitchen or something. And that will keep it away. Okay?"

"Okay," I said. The scratching suddenly started again. But this time, it wasn't coming from below us. This time, it was much closer. It was coming from our side of the door.

Plainly put, we screamed our heads off. We screamed more than I thought was humanly possible. We screamed in sync. And just as we were both taking huge breaths to start screaming all over again, we heard my father's voice from above us.

"Where are you?" he was calling.

"Dad!" I screamed. "We're down here. Behind the door. We're locked in! Please get us out!"

"Hurry!" shrieked Miranda.

There was silence for a moment.

"Dad!" I howled.

"I'm here," I heard him say, and his voice sounded much closer. "Just a minute."

I heard a click as the lock was pulled back, and a triangle of faint light was thrown on us as the door opened.

"Dad!" I shouted again, and hurled myself at him.

"Okay," he said, putting his arms around me. "It's okay. Are you both all right? How on earth did you get down here?"

He led us both back up the stairs and into the kitchen. I actually began to cry from relief.

"We were exploring," I sniffled. "We wanted to explore the secret staircase to the kitchen, and then we found out it kept going down."

"And we found a door," continued Miranda, "and Cristyn got the lock open, and we started to go down the stairs, but it was too dark for our little flashlight."

"So we started to go back," I said. "But the door slammed closed and locked us in!"

"What?" said my father.

"It's true!" said Miranda. "And we lost the flashlight, and we were there for, like, a half hour in total darkness, pounding on the door and screaming."

"The door just closed? Just like that?"

Miranda and I looked at each other. We couldn't tell the truth. My dad was a wonderful parent under almost any circumstances. But he was a man of facts. Period. I knew he'd never believe us.

"And then we heard mice," I added, "scratching, but we couldn't see anything and the noise kept getting closer . . ." I dissolved into tears again, and clung to my father's sweater like a toddler.

"Okay," said my father, stroking my hair gently. "Let's just calm down a bit, then we'll get everyone together, and we'll get to the bottom of this."

"Okay," I murmured.

"Okay," repeated Miranda.

8

My father continued pacing the length of the study.

"So what we have here," he said, "are two different stories. Dennis admits to pouring water on his sister's head when she was sleeping, and he admits to following you both into the woods and throwing pebbles at you."

"They were rocks," said Miranda.

"Were not!" said Dennis.

"However," my father continued, "Dennis denies taking the picture of your mother, Cris, and he denies locking you in the basement."

We couldn't very well argue. We had a pretty good idea by now that Dennis hadn't done those things. All we could do was to keep quiet and listen. And be thankful we hadn't mentioned the furniture being moved in our room. Anyway, Dennis had played some tricks. That much was true.

"Does anybody have anything to say here?" asked Mrs. Dunham.

"If Dennis says he didn't lock us in," I said quickly, "then I believe him. The door is old, and there was a draft. Maybe it just slammed shut, and the lock got stuck."

"I didn't do it," mumbled Dennis.

"Let's just forget about it," said Miranda, and her mother looked pleased.

"I agree," I said.

"Good," said Mrs. Dunham, smiling. "You know, I think if the three of you just work at it a little bit, you can all get along just fine."

Miranda and I both nodded, eager to have the subject put to rest.

"Okay, then," said my father. I became aware that Dennis was staring at me. I refused to look back at him. I didn't look at anyone, and I just stared at my shoes.

Oh, how I longed to hear Charlotte snap her gum.

Still shaken from the events of the morning, I felt a childish need to stay near my father all afternoon. He let me stay in the study where he and Mrs. Dunham were working. They had built a fire in the fireplace, and the room was cozy and warm. I lay on my stomach near the hearth, and wrote a long letter to

Charlotte. When I was done, I looked up Owain Glyndwr in the encyclopedia. I found out that in 1400 he led the Welsh in a revolt against the English, who had ruled Wales since the late thirteenth century. Owain had risen up against the English king because the English laws were unfair to the Welsh, and he had been successful for a number of years before finally being defeated. The book said he was considered one of the greatest national heroes of Wales.

My people, I thought to myself. This is my history. I have a history. Dad is writing his *magnopus* on my ancestors' greatest hero. I liked that idea. I felt in some way he could be doing it for my mother. I hoped so, anyway.

Dinner was a subdued affair, compared to the earlier excitement. Dad told some stories about Owain Glyndwr capturing English castles against enormous odds. He seemed really surprised but happy that I wanted to hear them. The stories were pretty interesting, though. Even Dennis got excited about Glyndwr's capturing Harlech Castle. He made my father tell it twice. In spite of everything he'd done to us, I couldn't help but feel a little affection for Dennis, being so nice to my dad and all, and acting all interested in his stories. I certainly hadn't made any efforts with Mrs. Dunham, but then again, she wasn't exactly approachable.

After dinner, I did the dishes, then went upstairs to join Miranda in our room. We hadn't been alone together since the conference in the study.

"So that came off pretty well, don't you think?" asked Miranda, curled at the foot of my bed.

"Well, we did accomplish our objective of getting out of the cellar without having to explain how we got locked in. I'm glad he didn't push it about the picture. He probably thinks I did it. I did feel bad about bringing Dennis into it, though."

"Don't. He's done plenty of other stuff that he hasn't gotten blamed for. It all, as they say, comes out in the wash. Anyway, we admitted it wasn't him in the end."

"We were right, though, weren't we? I mean, we can't tell them, right?"

"Would your father have believed us?" she asked.

"No," I said, a little sadly. "He's a class-A skeptic when it comes to stuff like ghosts and UFOs. He always gets really annoyed when people talk about it. I don't know what he would have thought, but he wouldn't have believed us. Unless they've seen stuff, too."

"Believe me, Cris, my mother hasn't seen anything. If she had, she'd be halfway home by now. She's terrified of stuff like that."

"Are you?" I asked suddenly.

"Terrified? Of course not. Nervous, possibly. Apprehensive, uncomfortable, and slightly grossed out. But not terrified. Terrified is for mothers."

"What are we going to do?" I asked.

"Sleep with the lights on again. Investigate the possibility of getting a very large dog."

"I'm serious," I said. "What are we going to do about it?"

"What can we do?" she asked. "Look up Ghost Control in the yellow pages, and have them come spray the house with spirit repellent?"

I laughed. "Come on, though. We have to think of something."

"No we don't. I can live with little noises and things moving around for the summer. I totally hate it, but I can live with it. But I'm certainly not going to go out of my way to talk to the thing. Get real."

"But don't you want to know what it means? Aren't you curious?" I asked.

"Not in the slightest. And even if I was curious, what would I do about it? Hunt down the people who used to live here and interrogate them?"

"No one used to live here. It's a rental."

"It is now, but it wouldn't always have been."

"It has been for a long time," I said, looking out the window.

"Why do you say that?" asked Miranda. I didn't answer her, because all of a sudden I was wondering if this had been my mother's room once, too.

"Cris? Hello? Why do you say it's been rented for a long time?"

"It's nothing, really," I said, turning to her. "It's just that, when we got here, my father thought he recognized the house from a painting my mother had. She left Wales with her family when she was ten, and she spent her last summer in this town. In a house that apparently looked a lot like this one."

"Oh, my God," Miranda said. "Did that freak him out?"

"I don't know," I replied. "I didn't exactly ask. I just kind of let the subject drop."

"Why?" she asked. "Aren't you curious? I mean, if she did stay here . . ."

"No," I said. "I mean, maybe sometimes I'm curious. But the thing is, Miranda, whenever her name comes up, which isn't often, he gets this look on his face. Like he's somewhere else. In a not very nice place. It's awful. It makes me feel so terrible. I mean, if that's what it's going to do to him, then why bring it up? She's gone for keeps. Talking about it would just make it worse."

"For him, or for you?" she asked.

"It's the same thing," I said. "So let's drop it."

"Okay. But just because the house has been rented out all this time doesn't mean it wasn't lived in."

I nodded. "That's true. I just wish I knew a way to find out what's happening here."

"Not me. If it wants something that badly, it's just going to have to figure out a way to tell us in plain English. But I just want it to leave us alone."

"I don't," I said. "I think it's exciting."

"Well," said Miranda, getting up and crossing to her own bed, "then you'd better get your own room, because I'd just as soon this one be left in peace."

And for that night, at least, it was.

9

Two days passed with no flying coins, moving furniture, or slamming doors. I ached for some excitement. Miranda and I amused ourselves by making collages of dream men from the scraps of old magazines. She refused, however, to extend any goodwill to Dennis or her mother, and seemed content to have settled us in our respective camps; herself and me against the world. It was weird, really, this idea she had about sides and stuff. She'd made it pretty clear in her own way that I was either with her, or against her. Dennis was cute and everything, but I didn't exactly see myself bonding with him and spending the next two months hand in hand, so I stuck with Miranda, even though I felt kind of guilty. I mean, Dennis had nobody. And I had told my father I would try with both of them. Still, what was I supposed to do?

Dad and Mrs. Dunham had insisted on going to

town, in spite of the fact that it had been pouring since breakfast. They invited us all to go along, and Dennis readily agreed, but Miranda declined the invitation, so I decided to stay home and keep her company, even though I was practically dying to get out of the house. Loyalty, or something. Anyway, Dolwyddelan would be there all summer.

We tried a little more halfhearted exploring of the house, but there really wasn't anything much of interest to see. We ended up going back to our room with my father's Scrabble board. Miranda was pretty good, and I enjoyed playing with her, so after the first game, we started another.

"Akin," said Miranda. "And, triple word score. Ha ha ha!"

"I'm not dead yet," I said, scanning my tiles for a good word.

"I hope they get back soon," said Miranda. "I am starving. Are you sure your father will remember my peanut butter?"

"He'll remember," I said, toying with some vowels. "He's real good about stuff like that."

"You're lucky," she said, and I smiled in agreement.

"He's kind of cute, too," she added, and I looked at her in surprise.

"Cute? My father? You must be kidding," I said.

"No, he is!" she protested. "The salt-and-pepper

hair, the short, clipped beard, the round glasses. Face it, Cris, he's cute."

"He's my father," I said. "Cute does not compute."

"It does for me," said Miranda, grinning. "After a week without television you start to notice things you might not notice otherwise!"

"Shut up," I said. "I'm trying to concentrate here."

She did shut up for a moment, and triumphantly I began to form the word *legends* on the board, chuckling with pleasure. I'd gotten the first four letters onto the board when I heard the sound of typing from the kitchen.

"They're back!" said Miranda, jumping to her feet. "Come on, I'm starving. We'll finish later."

A little reluctantly, I left my word unfinished, and followed Miranda. We ran down the main staircase, and bounded into the kitchen. The typing sound abruptly stopped as we came through the door. The kitchen was empty. We both stood silent, momentarily paralyzed.

"Mother?" called Miranda. "Dennis?" There was no response. I ran back into the hallway and opened the front door. The car was not in the driveway. I walked back into the kitchen.

"They're not here, Miranda," I said softly. "The car isn't back yet."

She just stood there, frozen in her tracks.

"Don't tell me you didn't hear it," I said. "I know you did."

"I heard it," she said weakly.

The typewriter was sitting on an old sewing table between the wood-burning stove and the door to the staircase. There was a piece of paper in it.

I walked toward the typewriter and reached for the paper, which was covered with letters, and pulled it out. I held it up for Miranda to see.

It read:

LLYWELYN LLYWELYN LLYWELYN LLYWE-LYN LLYWELYN LLYWELYN LLYWELYN LLYWELYN LLYWELYN LLYWELYN LLYWE-LYN LLYWELYN LLYWE

"Stop it!" said Miranda, covering her eyes.

"What does it mean?" I asked.

"Just throw it away," she said.

"Miranda, you said we couldn't do anything about it unless it figured out a way to tell us something. Well, this is something, isn't it?"

She uncovered her eyes, and looked nervously around the room.

"I thought terrified was just for mothers," I said.

"It is," she snapped.

"Then look at the paper," I commanded.

"I see it," she said.

"It's Welsh, isn't it?" I said, knowing somehow that it was. "Llywelyn is a Welsh name, I think. I know this name. You say it like Lou-Ellen, right?"

"Maybe," she said.

"We need to find out about this name," I pressed.

"Cris? Look, I saw it, you're right, it's telling us something. Okay? You win. But can we just, for now, can we just go back upstairs and finish the game, or something? Just until everybody gets back? Please?"

She was scared. More scared than I was. I folded the paper and put it into my pocket.

"All right," I said. "Come on."

There was no question of using the secret staircase. From the way Miranda's face had paled, I knew she'd be steering clear of there for a while. We walked through the main hall and back up the central staircase. Miranda heaved a big sigh as we reached the top of the stairs.

"Girl," she said, "I am glad to be out of that kitchen."

I followed her into our room, making little chicken noises to tease her. She didn't say anything at all. She just stood there, staring at the Scrabble board. I walked around her and took a look at it myself. All of our tiles had been wiped clean off the board. All of the letters were gone, except for seven that hadn't been there before. The seven remaining tiles were arranged across the center of the board. They spelled out a name: CRISTYN.

If Mrs. Dunham was surprised at Miranda's sudden desire to hang out with the rest of the family, she didn't show it. We lingered over the lunch table, getting my father to tell another Owain Glyndwr story. Miranda didn't speak to her brother or her mother, but she didn't give them any nasty looks, either.

Lunch, however, could not last forever.

"Miranda and I will wash up," I said.

"Thank you, sweetheart," said my father.

"Yes, that's very thoughtful," said Mrs. Dunham.

"Well, Erica, what do you say?" asked my father. "Ready to retreat to the Den of Doom for another battle against the reference texts?"

"I am if you are," she said, smiling. I think that was the first time I'd really seen her smile. She looked different. Nicer.

"Can I help make the fire?" asked Dennis, looking at my father eagerly.

"I was about to ask if you'd do just that," said my father. Dennis beamed and ran into the study, followed by his mother. The kid was certainly easy to please.

"All right, then," said my father. "Are you two okay?"

I nodded, and he gave me one of his dad smiles. "Give a knock if you need anything."

"Thanks," said Miranda. I gave him a little wave, and he walked out of the room.

"Here," I said, handing Miranda a towel. "You dry."

She worked in silence for several moments.

"Are you feeling better now?" I asked.

"Better? You mean, less freaked out?"

"Less freaked out, yeah," I said.

"I don't know," she replied. "Maybe. A little, I guess."

"What do you think it means?" I asked.

"I don't — I mean do you — I don't know, Cris."

"What were you going to say?" I asked.

"Nothing. Just, I mean, don't think I'm crazy or anything, but do you think maybe it's, like, your mother?"

I shook my head. "No way," I said firmly.

"Why?" she asked. "How do you know?"

"Can't say," I said. "I just know. I mean, I would know. If it were her. I — just trust me on this one. It isn't her."

"Then maybe the typing — maybe the person is this Lou-Ellen, whoever that is."

"That's what I was thinking," I said. "I just can't get it out of my head that the name sounds familiar, somehow."

"Not to me," Miranda said, drying the last of the dishes. "So what are we supposed to do about it?"

"I don't know," I said. "We need to know more about that name. Wait here a second."

I walked out of the kitchen toward the study, knocked gently on the door, and walked inside. Mrs. Dunham and my father were leaning over some notes together, and Dennis was sprawled by the fire.

"Dad?" I asked. "Would it be okay if Miranda and I borrowed the *Columbia Encyclopedia*?"

"Sure," he said, looking up from his work. "As long as you're prepared to surrender it at a moment's notice."

"No problem," I said, lugging the heavy book out the door. I brought it back to Miranda in the kitchen.

"Thank you so totally much for leaving me alone in here," she said, scowling.

"Why? Did something happen?"

"That's beside the point," she said, huffily. "Something could have happened. What are you doing?"

"Looking up the name 'Llywelyn,' " I said, leafing through the encyclopedia. "Okay, here we go. Llywelyn ap . . . I don't know how to say this one . . .

Iorwerth. It says he was a Welsh prince who fought against the English."

"When?" Miranda asked.

"Let's see, it says under his rule Welsh rights were recognized in the Magna Carta in 1215."

"Twelve fifteen?" Miranda asked. "No way. My mother said this house was built in, like, 1550 something."

"I heard it was built on top of something much older than that," I replied.

"Still . . . just because there was a Llywelyn around in 1215 doesn't mean our typist Llywelyn is any relation. I mean, if he was a big hero or something, probably a lot of people name their kids that, right?"

"Maybe," I said. "But there's something else here, Miranda."

"What?" she asked.

"Do you know what one of his main castles was called?"

She gave me an exasperated look.

"Sorry," I grinned. "Dolwyddelan. One of his castles was here."

"So?" Miranda said. "Then probably a lot of people in Dollwhatever call their kids Llywelyn."

"Maybe," I said reluctantly. "It's too bad, though. It would be pretty cool to be haunted by a Welsh prince, don't you think?"

"I don't know," said Miranda. "Is there a picture of him? Was he cute?"

I rolled my eyes and shut the book.

"I guess I should take this back," I said.

"Have fun," Miranda replied. I got up, but something came to me.

"Miranda, where's the coin?" I asked.

"In my pocket," she said.

"Let me see it for a sec." She reached into the pocket of her jeans, pulled it out, and handed it to me.

"I can't remember the date that was on here," I said, holding the coin up to the light. "Here it is — 1282. Oh."

"So much for your Welsh prince theory. He would have had to have been pretty old to still be alive in 1282," Miranda said.

I opened the encyclopedia again and turned back to the Llywelyn entry.

"Yup," I said. "Died 1240. Oh, well."

But instead of closing the book, I turned back a page. "Aha!" I said, triumphantly.

"Aha what?" said Miranda, leaning around me to survey the page.

"Another Llywelyn. Llewelyn ap Gruffudd. What does *ap* mean? See, it says he was ap Iorwerth's grandson. Another great Welsh prince. Where does it give dates?"

"Marriage by proxy in 1275," Miranda read. "What's marriage by proxy?"

"Does it say anything about Dolwyddelan?" I asked. "Let's look that up and see if it says — "

"Cris, look," said Miranda, pulling the book toward her so I couldn't.

"I can't see," I said.

"Llywelyn was separated from his troops after a battle and killed by an English soldier. In 1282."

We looked at each other.

"Looks like he's our man," I said.

10

After a brief discussion, we agreed that Llywelyn should remain a secret. It did sound pretty ludicrous, and it wasn't as if anyone else had actually heard that typewriter plunking away by itself. We could have typed the paper ourselves. So we said nothing. We were cautious and edgy throughout the night, but nothing out of the ordinary happened at all. The next morning, the first thing we noticed was that the rain had stopped. We had a feeling it would probably be a temporary thing, so we quickly put on our jackets and ran outside. The ground was soaked, and a heavy layer of fog lay over the landscape.

"Creepy," said Miranda.

"Let's go to the circle," I said quickly.

"Why?" Miranda asked. "We've seen it. Let's go explore in the other direction."

"You can if you want," I said. "I'm going to the circle before the rain starts again."

I started walking quickly toward the stone bridge, knowing Miranda would follow me. She could be kind of bossy, but she didn't seem the type to go off on her own. I didn't want to explain to her my compulsion to return to that place and probably couldn't have explained even if she asked. The desire to go back there had been in the back of my mind since we first discovered the circle, but with the heavy falling of rain, there had been no further opportunity.

"Wait up," Miranda called from behind me. "You're like an Olympic sprinter or something."

I hurried across the stone bridge, casting a quick glance back at the house. The fog was so thick, the house was completely invisible. The path was easy to find, though, and I stepped onto it, not caring about the mud that soon soaked my sneakers and socks.

"Cris," said Miranda, now closer behind me, "will you chill out? Before I have a heart attack?"

I slowed down a little bit and allowed her to catch up with me.

"Just chill out," she said again, but she didn't continue.

The circle looked wet and gray, but I was thankful the minute I walked into it. I picked a stone and sat down on it, breathing heavily. Miranda sat next to me.

"So what do we — " Miranda began, but I shushed her.

"I just want it to be quiet for a while," I said, and she didn't say anything further.

I took a deep breath and looked around me, seeing a strange beauty in the little stones that formed the rough circle. This was a peaceful, safe place, I felt. A good place. I took another deep breath, then a chill ran suddenly up my spine.

Miranda was sitting to my left. Though I was looking straight ahead, I could see her out of the corner of my eye. But very suddenly, I became distinctly aware of something more. The feeling grew more intense, and I suppressed a little shudder. I could feel another presence in the unexplainable way you sometimes know that someone is watching you. I was absolutely certain that there was another person sitting to my right, and that there were now three of us in the circle.

"Do you feel it?" I whispered to Miranda.

"What? Is it raining again?" she asked.

"There's someone else here," I murmured. "Don't you feel it?"

"Dennis!" shrieked Miranda, jumping up.

"Sit down," I hissed, grabbing her sleeve. "It's not Dennis."

"What do you mean?" said Miranda.

"Listen," I said. "Feel. Do you see? Can you tell?"

She was quiet for a moment, then said, "I think so."

I turned my head very slowly and looked toward my right. I could see nothing, but the feeling of the presence remained strong.

"Llywelyn," I whispered.

Nothing. No movement, just the feeling of a person, almost like heat, but alive.

"Llywelyn? Are you Llywelyn?"

And suddenly there was a little whispery noise, which could have been an answer, or could have been the sound of the rain falling through the trees around the circle. I realized it had been raining for almost a minute. I was getting wet but hadn't noticed.

Miranda grabbed me on the arm.

"Are you listening to me, Cristyn? Come on, let's go already!"

I pulled my arm out of her grasp and turned back to my right, but there was nothing. The feeling was completely gone.

"He's gone," I said.

"This is creepy," said Miranda. "Let's go. Come on, it's starting to pour again!"

I looked at the place again, but I knew he wasn't coming back. Not this time, this place. Miranda started down the path, and, not knowing what else to do, I followed her.

We were in the kitchen washing our muddy shoes and socks in the sink, when Mrs. Dunham came in. Her mouth dropped at the sight of us.

"What have you two been up to? You've tracked mud all over the kitchen."

"We'll clean it up," I said.

"Miranda, your brother has been alone all morning, when you know I had asked you to spend time with him."

"So what?" Miranda said, her face suddenly darkening.

"Miranda, back off," I muttered, but she ignored me.

"Don't speak to me that way, Miranda," said Mrs. Dunham. "I am still your mother."

"Not to me," Miranda muttered. "You're as bad a mother as you were a wife. It's no wonder he left!"

"You don't know anything about it, Miranda," her mother said in a dangerously soft voice.

"I know everything, Mother," Miranda snapped.

"You seem to keep forgetting that I'm part of the family! What was he supposed to do with you holed up in your office all of the time! The only reason you ever came out was to make us be quiet. You were a rotten wife! He was lucky he got away. I just wish he'd taken me with him."

"You have no idea what you're saying," said Mrs. Dunham. "You don't know the things — "

"You drove him away! He took work that would keep him in London half the time so he could get the hell away from you! Admit it! Admit it!" Miranda screamed.

"Does he call you? Does he write? Does he do anything for you?" Mrs. Dunham cried angrily.

"You made his life miserable just like you're making mine miserable. The only time you speak to me is to criticize, just like you did with him! The minute I get the chance, I'm going to get as far away from you as possible!"

With that, Miranda ran out of the room and up the stairs. Mrs. Dunham sat down heavily in a chair and put her head in her hands. Part of me wanted to go after Miranda. Maybe I could convince her to apologize or something. But something in the sight of Mrs. Dunham slumped in that chair made me stay. Not that I knew the background or anything, but Miranda had said some pretty rotten things. I mean, at least she *had* a mother.

"Um, can I get you anything?" I asked. Mrs. Dunham looked up like she was seeing me for the first time.

"Cristyn," she said softly.

"Is there something I can do? Something?" I said, feeling stupid.

"Does she talk to you?" she asked.

"You mean, about you?"

"About any of it," she said. "About me, Dennis. Her father."

"She's mad," I said. "She feels like you're favoring Dennis and ignoring her. Which, to be fair, it does kind of seem like you're doing."

Mrs. Dunham sighed. "I never thought that when he left, I might lose my children, too," she said. "But I almost lost Dennis, and as for Miranda . . . we don't even know each other anymore."

"What do you mean you almost lost Dennis?" I asked.

"I never told her," said Mrs. Dunham. "I haven't told anyone. Except your father."

"Told her what?"

She sighed, took off her glasses, and rubbed her eyes. She looked younger without her glasses. Kind of pretty, even. For a mother.

"He took Dennis. Michael, my ex-husband, did. There was this Little League game, and Dennis had been begging his dad to go. I told Miranda he left town after that game, but that's not the whole truth. He told Dennis they were going on a trip, so Dennis got in the car with him. They took the freeway out of town and drove about thirty or forty miles before Michael must have changed his mind about taking Dennis. They pulled into a gas station, and Dennis went into the bathroom. When he came out, his father was gone. I didn't hear from Michael for six months after that."

I stared at her in surprise. "Dad said there had been some . . . problem."

"The problem was attempted kidnapping. I asked him to keep it between the two of us."

"But how — what happened then?"

"The gas station manager called the police, and they took Dennis to the station. Dennis knew our address and phone number, and the police called me. I came and got him. And I lied to him. I told him Michael had asked me to meet them there to drive Dennis home, and that I'd forgotten."

"But . . . why didn't you tell Miranda? Why didn't Dennis say anything?"

"I — Michael was gone. I knew then that he didn't mean to come back. I didn't know how to explain it to her. She had been spending that day with a friend, so she really didn't know what had happened. I told Dennis I'd made a mistake forgetting to pick him up, and I asked him to keep it our secret."

"You didn't tell anyone? You didn't tell the police?" I asked.

She shook her head. "I didn't want Michael found. Cristyn, I was terrified. I couldn't think straight. Children are kidnapped by their own parents all the time. If he had really taken Dennis, I might never have seen him again. Michael does a lot of business in London. If they had left the country together . . . It just scared me to death. At that point, I didn't want Michael to come back. I didn't want the police, or anyone, looking for him. I just felt safer with him gone. I wouldn't let Dennis out of my sight after that, I was so afraid Michael would change his mind again and come back for him. Miranda's right — I guess I have been favoring Dennis all this time, but I did it because I was afraid."

"But why . . . I mean, why did you keep all this from Miranda?"

"In spite of what you heard Miranda say to me, part of her knows that her father was no saint. As she kept saying, she was there. He was gone a lot of the time, and when he was home he sometimes drank too much. He could be mean. There were times when he was very difficult, and there were times when he was delightful. And when he was happy, we all were. Miranda knows what went on.

And she knows that since Michael left town, he has never tried to contact her or Dennis for any reason. That's got to hurt them both very deeply. I just felt . . . I just wanted her to be able to keep some good memories of him. I didn't want her to know what a terrible thing he'd done. Tell me, Cristyn, what kind of man would abandon his seven-year-old son in a gas station in the middle of nowhere? I just didn't want either of them to know he was capable of that. And to be honest, how do you think Miranda would have felt knowing her father tried to take Dennis, but not her?"

"Yeah," I said. "But you get to be blamed, now."

"I know. I've often wondered if I was wrong to keep it from her. Finally, I broke down and told Derek the whole story. I had to tell someone. He's obviously such a wonderful father, and I really value his advice."

"What did he say?"

"He felt that Miranda should, at some point, know the truth, but that given her current state, now is probably not the best time. And I think he's right. I will tell her someday, but not now. Not with things as they are. Derek is right. That would do more harm than good."

"If this is such a big secret and everything, why did you tell me?"

She gave me a long look.

"Your father loves you so much, Cristyn, he talks about you all the time. I got to feeling like I knew you almost as well as he did. I feel like I can trust you. And you'll be spending so much time with Miranda, now, when it's so crucial that we be a family again. I just thought it might help, somehow, if you knew. I know she's being moody, and that isn't making things easy on you. I'm sorry you had to hear us saying those things to each other. It must be unpleasant for you, being stuck in the middle. But maybe you can understand a little better where things stand, and be of some help to her. Somehow. I don't know."

"I just think you should tell her, that's all," I said. "In spite of what Dad said."

"She won't believe me. She'll be angry."

"How much angrier can she get, Mrs. Dunham?" I asked, and she smiled a little.

"I'll think about it, Cristyn. I will. In the meantime, you won't say anything?"

I nodded, and then she really smiled. A big, motherly kind of a smile. I envied Miranda her mother at that moment.

That night, I dreamed about Miranda and her mother fighting in the kitchen, but then I was outside the house. I saw the same horse I had dreamed about the first night I'd come to Wales, but this time there was a girl on it, and the man from my first dream wasn't there. It was one of those dreams where you're both doing something and watching yourself do it at the same time. The girl that was/was not me jumped onto the horse's back. There was a thick fog around everything, and the horse was rearing frantically. The girl/me shouted and kicked the horse, and they/we galloped off as the fog swirled and danced. There was another noise, too, something familiar, but I couldn't quite pinpoint what it was.

II

Miranda and I both slept late the next morning. My father, who obviously knew exactly what had gone on between Miranda and her mother, brought toast and juice to our room. I looked out at the gray sky and munched on my toast.

"Another rotten day," said Miranda from her bed. "I feel lousy. I think I have a cold."

I wiped some crumbs off my mouth. "You know," I said, "you said some pretty mean things to your mom last night. If you tried talking to her you might — "

"Cris, I don't want to talk about it. Not with you, not with my mother, not with my shrink, not with anyone. Get it?" Her face screwed up, and I thought she was about to cry, but she sneezed instead.

"Bless you," I said, not really meaning it, and she moaned a little.

"I knew I was going to get sick," she said. "My life sucks."

"So what about yesterday, though?" I said, changing the subject. "At the circle. That was him, don't you think? I mean, there was something there, Miranda; it was definitely a person. I think he must have been Llywelyn, don't you?"

"I guess," Miranda said, screwing up her face for another sneeze that didn't come.

"I couldn't see him, though," I said. "I could just tell somebody was there. I wish I could have seen him."

"Yeah," said Miranda, sinking back against her pillows.

"So how are we going to contact him?" I asked. "How are we going to find out what he wants?"

"How do you know he wants something?" asked Miranda.

"Because he's haunting us," I said. "That's why it happens. You know, like someone was murdered or something and they want to be avenged."

"But we know how he died," she said. "Soldiers killed him."

"But there could be something else," I said. "Something he didn't get to do, or something."

"Maybe," she said.

"I just wish I knew how to speak to him," I said.

"You don't speak Welsh," Miranda said. That was true.

I started to say something, but Miranda put her finger to her lips, and pointed at the little door to the secret staircase. It was very slightly opened.

"Yes, you're right," I said, moving casually toward the door. "I don't speak Welsh. But maybe Llywelyn — "

I jerked the door open suddenly, to reveal Dennis's startled face. Miranda shouted and threw a pillow at him, but it landed several feet short of its target. Dennis ran down the stairs and out of my sight.

"He's impossible!" shouted Miranda. "No one is safe!"

I shut the little door all of the way and returned Miranda's pillow to her.

"Oh, well," I said. "It's not like he had any way of knowing what we were talking about."

"Don't fool yourself," said Miranda angrily. "He's probably been eavesdropping since day one. He's probably at this very minute gloating to my mother that I believe in ghosts."

"Well," I said, taking Miranda's plate, "I'll just take these downstairs and see what he's up to."

"Smack him on the head," commanded Miranda. "Hard. Tell him it's from me."

"Whatever," I said, and headed downstairs.

Dennis was still in the kitchen when I got there. He looked a little frightened to see me.

"I'm sorry," he said quickly. "I didn't mean to, honest. I was exploring the staircase and I heard you talking. I just listened for a minute. I never did it before, honest."

He really did look frightened, and his wide-eyed expression melted my heart a little.

"Your sister's pretty mad," I said.

"I know," he replied. "She's always mad at me now."

"So why do you keep doing stuff to her? Why do you keep playing tricks?"

He shrugged. "Otherwise she doesn't talk to me at all," he said.

"Oh," I said.

"Are you mad at me, too?" he asked.

"Not really, no," I said, and he got that big pea-burbling smile on his face.

"Thanks, Cristyn," he said.

"It's okay," I replied and partially turned to leave.

"It's not a guy, you know," he said, and I turned back to face him.

"What?" I asked.

"It's not a guy. It's a girl."

"Who's a girl?" I asked.

"You know," he said. "The one who does stuff, makes stuff move. She's a girl."

He looked totally serious.

"How do you know?" I asked him.

"I've seen her," he said. "Two times."

"When?" I asked.

"Once in the kitchen, and once in the cellar."

"You went into the cellar?" I asked. "By yourself?"

"Sure," he said. "It's cool down there. I went again yesterday with your dad. After you got locked in. He wanted to explore. I didn't see her that time, though."

"Then who is Llywelyn?" I asked. I took the folded piece of paper out of my jeans pocket and showed it to him. "This was on the typewriter. It typed itself when you guys went into town."

"She did it, I bet," he said, looking at the paper. "I don't know who that is. It isn't her."

"But — what does she look like?" I pressed.

"She looks a little like you," he said, "but shorter. And her hair is very curly. She's pretty," he added softly.

"Dennis, if you're making this up — "

"I'm not!" he said, looking straight at me, and I believed him.

"What is she doing here? Who is she?" I asked.

"I don't know," said Dennis. "I think she lives in the cellar. Your dad said it was really old down there, that it was left over from another house. He said you can see where one of the rooms was, under the stairs. So maybe she's from a really long time ago."

"A coin fell in our room, from out of nowhere," I said. "It had the date 1282 on it."

"Twelve eighty-two," Dennis repeated. "Neat."

"Did she say anything to you, Dennis?"

He shook his head. "I talked, but she didn't say anything back. I think," he said, looking up into my face, "that she wants you."

"You what?" Miranda spluttered, brandishing a box of tissues at me.

"He knew already, Miranda," I said. "I just filled him in on the details. He knew everything else."

"You idiot!" she cried. "Don't you realize what he did? He listened to us talking, and he made the rest of it up. It's a prank, Cristyn, and you totally fell for it!"

"I don't think so," I said.

"You didn't think at all!" she cried. "You just blabbed it all out to him. My God, Cristyn, he's going to go straight to my mother, and she'll probably punish me for telling scary stories or something. You are so naive!"

"Fine," I said, beginning to grow irritated. "If you're so sure he's making it up, then there's only one thing to do. We'll go down into the cellar and see what happens. He said she lived there, and it *is* the oldest part of the house."

Miranda blew her nose furiously. "I cannot believe," she said, "how stupid you are being. It's a trick, Sherlock, to make us look like idiots. Like, how retarded are you?"

That really was enough. I stood up quickly.

"Your moods are really wearing thin," I said. "It would have been nice to have someone to hang out with this summer, but I tell you, Miranda, I'd much rather hang out by myself than get ragged on by you all day. You're the biggest baby I've ever met. You think the whole world revolves around you. Your life is nothing but a huge pity party that you're throwing for yourself. If you think I'm going to be impressed by the way you treat your mother and your brother, think again. It's pathetic, and so are you!"

"Oh, please!" Miranda cried, rolling her eyes. "My brother is a runt, and my mother is a complete nightmare. I wish she was dead!"

"I hate you!" I shouted, turning to go, trembling in anger at what she'd just said. My father was just going to have to understand that I couldn't play peacemaker with this little hysteric anymore.

"So I suppose you're going to go play with the stupid little scuz now?" she called quickly.

"He's your brother, Miranda. And speaking of stupid, has it occurred to you that you shouldn't tell me you wish your mother was dead? Did that enter your mind? Sherlock?" And I slammed the door on my way out, just for effect.

12

Dennis was waiting in the kitchen when I came back down.

"She's really mad now, right?" he asked.

"Right," I said, pouring myself a glass of orange juice. "But so am I. I have to admit, I was getting a little sick of your tricks, kiddo, but now I'm beginning to understand why you do it."

I expected Dennis to look pleased with himself, or to start dishing on his sister in a big way, but he didn't. He just stood there.

"So you think this girl is really down there?" I asked, taking a long sip of orange juice. Dennis nodded gravely.

"Then how come my dad didn't see her when he went down there?"

"She wants you," said Dennis.

"Why do you keep saying that?" I asked. "If she

didn't speak to you, how do you know she wants me?"

"She just does," said Dennis. "I just know."

I looked at him for a moment, then refilled my glass with juice. I was wondering if he could possibly know about my name being spelled out on the Scrabble board, but he'd been out of the house when that had happened. Miranda had been so freaked out by it that we hadn't really discussed it further, so I could rule out the possibility that Dennis had heard us talking about it. Of all things that had happened in the house, the Scrabble thing scared me the most. There was something chilling about seeing my name like that, and realizing that it wasn't just me watching the house. Something in the house was watching me. And it seems I'd been chosen. But for what?

"Dennis, what do you think she wants?" I asked, but he just shrugged. "Then what do I do?"

"Go down," he said.

"Go down. Just like that."

"It's just a room. You can't really see anything, just the dirt floor. Your dad said the first house would have been made from wood and stuff, not stone like this one. He said he'd have to spend a lot of time if he wanted to find any art fix."

"Artifacts," I corrected.

"Yeah."

"I don't have a light. We lost ours when . . . when we were on the stairs."

"I have it," said Dennis. "I got it back."

"I don't know, Dennis," I said. "You're not really supposed to poke around old places. It isn't safe, or whatever."

"Your dad let me," Dennis said, shifting from one small foot to another.

Okay, in truth I was just scared. I wanted to know this person who knew my name and made things go bump in the night, but I was afraid. Afraid of her, afraid of what I might find out, and afraid I might not find out anything.

"Cristyn," said Dennis, "I can go with you. You wouldn't have to be scared then, 'cause I could protect you."

I really, really didn't want to go down there. I wanted there to be some other way to contact her. But Dennis looked so eager. I wanted him to feel important for a little while. And I needed to know who she was. He's eight years old, I thought, and he went down there alone. I can do this.

"Okay," I said to Dennis, and his face brightened into a sweet smile. "Get the light."

He scrambled up the stairs, and I stood alone in the kitchen, waiting nervously. If this is a trick, I thought, I will personally pull each and every curly hair out of Dennis's head. But in my heart, which was pounding rapidly, I knew it was no trick.

Once again, the dead bolt slid back easily under my hands. I pulled the heavy door toward me and felt a blast of cool air in my face. A small hand slipped into mine, and Dennis led me through the door, shining the flashlight down the stairs.

"It's not very deep," he said as we descended one step at a time. "But your dad said to be careful, 'cause the steps are kind of slippery."

I kept my gaze firmly on my feet, where Dennis's flashlight illuminated each step as my foot touched it. I would not allow myself to look further, into the inky black where I'd heard those scratching sounds before. Suddenly, I stepped onto something soft. Dirt.

"This is the bottom," said Dennis. "See, look."

He shined the light in an arc from left to right. The space was about the size of the kitchen upstairs. There was nothing that I could see to show that a house had once stood on the spot. I could barely distinguish between the dark of the floor and the dark of the cellar wall.

"There's nothing here," I said. "It's just a hole."

Dennis pointed the flashlight to the ground. "There's a kind of ditch over there. Your dad said it was where one side of the house ended, maybe."

I couldn't see anything and pulled back a little as Dennis led me to the center of the room.

"Well, I'm here," I said, feeling a little foolish about the fact that I was still holding Dennis's hand. "But nothing seems to be happening."

I sensed the movement out of the corner of my eye at the same time Dennis made a gesture with his free hand toward the back of the room. My heart began beating wildly, and I squeezed Dennis's hand even harder, but I slowly made myself turn in the direction of the movement, in the hollow underneath the stairs. I closed my eyes until I had turned completely. Then I opened them, and that's when I saw her for the first time.

It's hard to describe exactly what it was like. You wouldn't have mistaken her for a living person, or anything. I mean, she definitely wasn't real, or alive, or whatever. But she wasn't like this white, see-through thing, either, like the ghosts you'd see on *Scooby-Doo*, or *Ghostbusters*. It was almost like a movie was being projected onto the wall. It flickered a little and looked a little wrong, but it was whole. She was whole.

She was standing by something that hadn't been there when Dennis shone the light, a table or something. She was leaning over it, doing something with her hands. It seemed like she might be preparing a meal. As Dennis had said, she was a little shorter than me, with dark curly hair and fair skin, and she looked to be about my age. She was barefoot, and wore a long, sleeveless tunic belted at the waist, and a kind of long-sleeved undershirt. Her hair hung in her face as she worked. She didn't seem to see Dennis or me at all. The back of her dress was sort of glowing, like there was a fireplace or a torch directly behind her. She straightened and pushed her hair out of her face with one hand. It seemed like she was waiting for something, expecting something.

I made a noise in my throat. I didn't exactly get a word to come out, but I definitely made a sound. She didn't respond or look at me.

"Can she see us?" I whispered to Dennis. He shook his head.

Then, for a moment, I thought she did see us. She turned in our direction and seemed to be staring right at me. But she wasn't looking at me. She was looking, not through me, but beyond me. I turned and looked in the same direction, but I saw nothing but blackness. When I turned back, I saw the look of disappointment on her face. Whatever, or whoever, she was waiting for was not there. She stood for a moment, looking a little crestfallen, then she turned and walked briskly past the table and out of sight. It was like she was on television, and when she walked offscreen, the television switched off.

Dennis and I were staring into the dark, the flashlight hanging down by his side.

"What happened?" I asked. "Where is she?"

"I don't know," said Dennis. We waited a few minutes, but nothing else happened.

"I guess that's it then," I said, and Dennis just shrugged. He didn't seem at all amazed or scared by what had happened. I guess it's easier to just take what comes when you're eight. Not me, though. I was full of questions.

We walked back up the stairs, carefully locked the door (as if it could keep her in), and went into the kitchen. There was no sign of Miranda.

"Do you want some hot cocoa or something?" I asked Dennis, and he nodded and gave me one of his girlish smiles.

"Is that what you saw before?" I asked, filling the kettle up with water.

"She didn't do much before," said Dennis, "and she was only there a little. Took much longer today."

I placed the kettle on the stove. "But she didn't seem to know we were there, or anything. I mean, if she wants something, she's gonna have to tell me what it is, right?"

"I guess," said Dennis. "Make it with half milk, half water, okay?"

"Then how am I going to find out what's going on?"

"I like it extra chocolatey," said Dennis, handing me the cocoa tin.

"Dennis?"

"We can go again tomorrow and wait for her," he said, still holding out the tin.

It seemed like the thing to do, since I didn't have a Ouija board or a crystal ball. I took the cocoa from Dennis and stirred it into a mug of steaming milk and water. I kept stirring long after the cocoa had dissolved, lost in thoughts of the girl with pale skin and dark eyes, waiting for something, waiting for someone.

13

The four of us were laughing so hard we almost knocked the dinner plates right off the table.

"I'm not making it up," said my father, still giggling. "I swear it! I just can't remember where I read it, or who it was about!"

"Derek, don't you think I'd know it if one of the kings of England died from eating too many stewed lampreys?" said Mrs. Dunham, causing me to start laughing all over again.

"What's a lamprey?" asked Dennis. The fact that he had no idea what we were talking about hadn't prevented him from joining in the merrymaking.

"Kind of a snakey-looking fish," said my father, still grinning. "It's true, Erica. One of those Plantagenet kings had a real passion for stewed lampreys, and it finally did him in!"

"Well, it wouldn't be the worst death ever suffered by an English royal," Mrs. Dunham said.

"No, I think the award for Most Gruesome Death of a King or Queen of England goes to Edward II," my father said, spearing a leek on the end of his fork.

"What?" cried Dennis, who was already exhibiting symptoms of becoming guts-obsessed.

"Never mind," said Mrs. Dunham, giving my father a look. He just grinned.

"What?" said Dennis again. "What happened to him?"

I lifted the bowl of steamed leeks into the air. "Stewed lamprey, anyone?" I asked, and my father cracked up all over again. It was so good to see him laughing that way. He fell apart all over again when Dennis grabbed two of the celery-shaped leeks and stuck them on his head.

"Look, I'm a bug!" shouted Dennis, making his eyes bulge out. I expected his mother to tell him to stop, but she just gave him an affectionate look and rolled her eyes a little. It was then that Miranda walked into the kitchen in her bathrobe and slippers.

"There she is," said my father. "Feeling any better?"

"Not really," said Miranda, pouring herself a glass of orange juice.

"Anything we can get for you?" my father pressed. "Anything you need?"

"Yeah," said Miranda, turning to face him. "It'd be real nice if you guys could keep it down in here. Not to spoil your party, or anything, but I'm sick, after all."

She took her glass of orange juice and walked out of the kitchen. If I was mad at Miranda before, I was twice as mad now. Who did she think she was, talking to my father that way? My father, who seemed to be genuinely enjoying himself for the first time since I could remember. My father, who was trying to be nice to her, when she'd done nothing to deserve it. Where did Miranda get off talking to him like that?

Mrs. Dunham must have seen the look on my face.

"She didn't mean that the way it sounded," she said apologetically. "She's probably getting a little lonely, lying up there and listening to us all laughing in here."

"It's no fun being sick," my father said, pouring himself a glass of wine. "I can't blame her for being grumpy."

But I could. I didn't go upstairs until I was ready to go to bed, and when I did, Miranda and I didn't speak to each other. We didn't even look at each other.

I had the dream about the girl on the horse again, but this time I could see the girl's face. It wasn't me on that horse. It was the girl from the basement, and she looked terrified.

Miranda stayed in bed the next morning, and I gladly left her there. When Dad got the mail, he found a letter for me from Charlotte, which I eagerly took down to the stone circle and read. The sight of her large, rounded handwriting filled me with homesickness.

Charlotte reported that Geoff, my Geoff, had asked Charlotte about me several times. She also reported that he was not going out with anybody else. Yet. I rolled my eyes at the "yet" — typical Charlotte. There was a long section about a Debbie somebody who had stolen a Calvin Klein sweater from another girl. Charlotte was particularly enraged about this. She ended the letter with a big lipstick mark on the bottom of the page, which had smudged so that it looked like a small blot of fluorescent pink blood. I read the letter over a couple of times, then folded it and put it in my pocket.

It was so peaceful in the stone circle. The sky was overcast, and it was a little chilly, but dry. I felt no unearthly presence, however. Whatever I had felt or sensed the other day was not in the circle now. I did, however, hear footsteps coming down the path, and Dennis's voice calling my name.

"Cristyn?" he called. "It's Dennis — I'm coming. I'm not playing a trick, okay?" he called.

I smiled to myself. Dennis had been working pretty hard to win my trust.

"Okay," I called back, catching sight of his blue windbreaker through the trees.

"Hi," he said, coming into the circle. "Is it okay? I could go."

"It's okay," I said, smiling. "Stay."

He smiled back at me and reached into his pocket.

"I brought you something," he said, handing me an orange.

"Thanks," I said, touched. "Want to split it?"

"Okay," he said. I started peeling it.

"Miranda still won't talk to me," he said, chewing on his lower lip.

"She won't talk to me, either," I said. "Can't say I'm sorry, though."

"I am," he said, and I wished I hadn't said it.

"She'll come around, Dennis," I said. "You know, sometimes you just get real mad at everybody, and it's hard to stop. But she will."

"She's been mad for a really long time," he said, toying with a piece of orange peel.

"It doesn't mean she doesn't love you," I said, handing him a section of orange.

"My dad left me in a gas station," he said suddenly, and I looked at him in surprise.

"Oh," I said stupidly. "I mean, your mom said something about that. She was late picking you up."

"No she wasn't. He was taking me away with him, but then he didn't want me anymore, so he left me there."

"Dennis, your mom told me all about it and she said — "

"She made it up. It's okay. She just didn't want me to be sad. But I knew it wasn't a mistake. He left me." He sucked thoughtfully on a piece of orange.

"He was mad at me like Miranda's mad now. She's gonna leave, too, I bet."

"Dennis," I said sharply, and he looked up at me. "Listen to me. I know this is difficult to understand, but the way your dad and your sister feel about stuff is not your fault. Okay? I know your sister loves you, and I'm sure your dad does, too. You didn't do anything wrong. Okay, Dennis? Trust me on this one. Please?"

"Okay," he said, not meeting my eye. I wanted to throttle Miranda at that moment. But part of me knew that Miranda had demons of her own. She was only partly to blame. I watched Dennis munch on the orange.

"Hey," I said. "Wanna go back downstairs and see what we see?"

"Dunno," he said, still not meeting my gaze.

"Well, I'll tell you, Dennis," I said, "I'd really like to go back down, but I'm kind of afraid to go without you."

"Yeah?" he said, finally looking at me.

"Yeah," I said, seeing a ghost of a smile on his face.

"I could go, then," he said, getting up. "Don't worry, Cristyn. I'll hold your hand again."

"Thanks, buddy," I said. I wonder if he knew I meant it.

When we got to the bottom of the stairs, Dennis switched off the flashlight.

"Why?" I shrieked.

He squeezed my hand. "It's okay," came his voice from the darkness. "We can see better this way."

I felt disoriented in the blackness, no longer sure which way was up. Then I sensed a flickering light, and I turned toward it. She was there again, in the space under the stairs, looking just as we'd left her.

"She's back," I murmured, and Dennis nodded.

She was running her hands through her hair and smoothing her tunic, as if she were expecting a visitor. She kept casting glances in our direction, but I knew now that she was looking at something else. A door.

Suddenly, her face lit up. She smiled, and in the change of expression she was suddenly wild and beautiful. Someone else walked into the picture. He was a tall, powerfully built man with graying hair, dressed in a long, flowing tunic. He was the most handsome man I'd ever seen.

"Carwen," he said as she threw her arms around him. "Carwen."

"Carwen," I repeated softly. "We finally know her name."

He drew back slightly from Carwen and took her hands in his own, examining her face. He spoke to her softly with musical, tangled sounds that I knew were the Welsh language. She laughed as he spoke, her eyes watching him intently. She asked a question every now and then, but she didn't seem to say much else. She just stared and stared at him with this incredible look of devotion on her face.

As I watched the two of them watch each other, still clasping hands, I realized what their relationship must be.

"He's her father," I whispered.

Carwen asked another question, and her father looked away, then shook his head. Her face fell, and she drew back from him. Her father turned in my direction, and the expression on his face, which I could now see was lined with age, grew dark.

"*Na*, Dad," Carwen whispered, and he came back to her. When they hugged, I looked away, suddenly embarrassed to be eavesdropping, even though I couldn't understand what they were saying. I looked back at them, though, because I knew that somehow all of this was being shown to me for a reason.

Carwen's father pulled away first, and he stroked his daughter gently on the cheek.

"*Pob hwyl,* Carwen," he said, then walked swiftly away. Carwen stood, looking after him, touching the place on her cheek where his hand had been. Then, very softly, she began to cry.

"Carwen," I called, but she didn't look up. She looked suddenly to the left, as if she'd heard something. Wiping the tears off her face, she walked away, and Dennis and I were alone in the dark.

It seemed like Carwen had been waiting for her father for a long time. They were obviously terribly fond of each other, but there was also something wrong. When he left, I got the feeling that he would not return right away. He didn't belong in that room with Carwen. He belonged somewhere else.

14

Saturday brought that rarest of jewels, a Welsh day without a cloud in the sky. Dad was so excited he called an official halt to research and announced it was the perfect opportunity to journey to the top of the famous Mount Snowdon. We wolfed down breakfast, then the four of us bundled into the tiny car. Miranda, predictably, said she was too sick and refused to join us.

The Snowdon train station was in a little town called Llanberis. Dad, Dennis, and I stood outside the station while Mrs. Dunham went in to buy tickets. She'd insisted loudly, over my father's protests, that the outing was "her treat," which I thought was sort of sweet in a mom kind of a way. Dennis was practically out of his head with excitement, running back and forth shouting "choo choo!" at the top of his lungs. I was pretty psyched, too, until I saw the train.

"Are they serious?" I asked. "It looks like a toy!"

"It's gonna be great, Cris," said my father, putting his arm around my shoulder.

"Dad, it's tiny! We're supposed to go up the highest mountain in Wales in that little thing? They sell bigger trains at toy stores. It can't be safe."

"It's safe," he beamed, giving me a hug. "Why do you worry so much?"

"Because I watch the news, Dad. I know the kinds of things that happen to people in rickety vehicles on mountains. They'll carry us out of there on bright orange stretchers, I just know it."

I was ready to launch into a whole dissertation about the wide range of injuries we were likely to sustain, but Dennis appeared suddenly at my elbow, and I didn't want to encourage him with talk of crushed skulls and broken bones.

"Mom, come on!" he cried in anguish. "It's gonna leave without us! Mom, come on!"

Mrs. Dunham jogged out of the station, waving four tickets triumphantly over her head, looking as pleased with herself as if she'd just captured Harlech Castle single-handedly.

"The last four tickets for the ten A.M. train!" she shouted.

"Well done!" my father said, in a pretty bad attempt at an English accent. "Here's to the organizational skills of the incomparable Erica Dunham!"

Dennis was so frantic he was actually leaping up and down, flapping his hands like a flightless bird.

"Okay, okay!" Mrs. Dunham said, laughing, and Dennis raced to the platform.

The train was divided into little compartments, and we clambered into one and peered out the windows at the station. I agonized over not being able to shut our door properly, until a uniformed man came and, from the outside, latched it tightly.

"Great," I muttered. "What if we need to get out?"

There was a slight lurch, and a great hiss of escaping steam, then the train pulled out of the station and began its slow ascent up the mountain.

It wasn't very interesting at first, just trees and houses, and the usual throngs of sheep, staring at us with wide, unblinking eyes. After ten or fifteen minutes, though, the rest of the landscape seemed to fall away as the mountain grew steeper. I gripped the edge of my seat slightly, but as the spectacular scenery unfolded around us, I refrained from closing my eyes. The mountain all around us was grassy and covered with rocks of all shapes and sizes. The farms below grew smaller and smaller, and the resident sheep shrunk into tiny beige dots.

I leaned past my father to look out his window and was astonished to see, far over the peak of a nearby mountain, a figure suspended from a little parachute, floating about on the air currents.

"What is he doing?" I asked, completely amazed. "Is he parachuting? Why is he just floating around?"

My father turned in the direction I was looking.

"He's para-gliding," said my father. "It's kind of a cross between parachuting and hang gliding."

"Now that is sick," I said firmly.

"Can we do that?" said Dennis eagerly. "Mom, can we para-glide? Can we?"

"Dennis," I said quickly, "you know you're my buddy. But if you even use the word *para-glide* in a sentence one more time, I'm going to throw up. Possibly all over you."

"Cool," said Dennis, but he dropped the subject. Mrs. Dunham flashed the thumbs-up sign and mouthed, "I owe you."

"Look," said my father. "You can see the top! We're almost there!"

The train let out a little groan as if to say we might not actually make it.

"I think I can I think I can," I muttered.

"What?" said Dennis.

"*The Little Engine That Could,*" I said, and he looked mystified. "Don't you know — don't they read that anymore? What is happening to our school system?" My father roared with laughter at that, for some reason. Before I could quite figure it out, the train shuddered to a halt, and we waited, helpless, for the uniformed man to reappear and free us from our windowed prison.

As soon as the door was opened, Dennis leaped out and took off up the path to the official "peak."

"Dennis!" Mrs. Dunham shouted, a little frantically. My father put his hand on her wrist.

"Erica," he said softly, "he'll be fine. Don't worry."

She may have given him a smile. I'm not sure. I couldn't take my eyes off my father's hand covering Mrs. Dunham's wrist. It occurred to me that I had never actually seen my father touch anyone like that before, in that kind of small, gentle way. Anyone but me, that is.

"Come on, Cris," said my father, stepping out of the compartment. "You're not going to sit in here the whole time, are you? We only have a half hour until the train goes back down — let's go!"

I climbed out of the train and stood on the rocky surface next to the two of them. A blast of wind hit my face, and I was surprised at how cold it was. Freezing, actually.

"Hey," my father said, taking my hand. "Let's go up to the peak, okay?"

I nodded, and we walked up the impossibly steep path together. Mrs. Dunham was already on her way up, keeping a wary eye on Dennis. It only took us a minute or two to reach the little monument at the peak, but my leg muscles were already screaming for mercy. Clambering up the last few rocks, I slapped my hand onto the monument, breathing heavily.

"Don't feel too sorry for yourself," said my father from behind me. "Some of these people actually hiked up from the bottom!"

I looked around at the hikers with a mix of disgust and admiration.

"I'm going to go sit on that flat rock," I said, pointing, and my father nodded as I made my way down. In truth, I was actually too scared to really look around me until I was planted firmly on something solid. Once settled safely on my rock, I looked around in amazement.

The sky was still virtually cloudless, and the view was astonishing. Below, I could see two large, deeply blue lakes at the foot of another mountain. The mountains loomed up below me, one after another, as far as I could see. The sight of them was comforting and lonely at the same time. I could see no towns, though I knew they must be there, nestled into the sides of the mountains like children pressing into their mothers.

It was almost silent, but the sound of the wind rushing over the rocks was better than silence. I could understand why people always think of heaven as being up in the sky. There was something safe about being up here, something timeless. It could be any year at all, I thought, staring out over land. Things must have looked just this way in 1282. From my mountain perspective, nothing had changed. The centuries had done nothing to Wales at all, had not worn away a bit of it.

This is Wales, I thought, gazing over all of it as a strange lump formed in my throat. I couldn't pinpoint exactly what I was feeling as I looked down over the landscape, but some mix of grief and happiness spilled in tears out of my eyes. I rubbed the wetness into my cheeks. Maybe I was crying for the lost Welsh girl, dead now for many years. But which Welsh girl? Carwen, or my mother?

I jumped as I felt a hand on my arm.

"Cristyn?" said Dennis. "Are you okay?"

"Sure," I said in a fake, bright way.

"You look like you're crying," he said softly.

"It's the wind," I said, smiling. "It's making me bleary-eyed."

He nodded. "We have to go down now. We're not allowed to stay here."

"No, I guess we're not," I said, and I followed him back to the train.

15

Early the next morning, my dad went back to the library, and returned with a fresh, grimy pile of books, which he hauled into the study. Miranda and I didn't speak at all, as she assumed I was now fully in Dennis's corner. She hadn't shaken her cold yet and didn't even get out of bed. She just lay there like a corpse, surrounded by mountains of tissues, her face obscured by a magazine.

I went down to the study to visit with Dad and Mrs. Dunham. Dennis was already there, poking at the fire. He grinned when he saw me.

"Para-glide para-glide para-glide," he sang, and beamed happily as I clutched my stomach and made little retching noises.

"Cristyn," said Mrs. Dunham softly, "I want you to know I really appreciate your spending so much time with Dennis. I wish there were more for you to do. I didn't realize you'd all be housebound so much of the time."

"Oh, we're having a great time," I said loudly enough for Dennis to hear.

"We were exploring," said Dennis.

"Exploring what?" asked him mother.

"The cellar, where the old house was," he replied. I gave him a look, which he didn't return. I truly hoped he wasn't about to blab the whole Carwen story. It hadn't occurred to me to tell him it was a secret. I'd been thinking of Carwen constantly, trying to piece together her mystery. It was too soon, though. I needed more pieces of the puzzle, and she hadn't given them to me. Yet.

"By yourselves?" said Mrs. Dunham. "I'm not sure I like the idea of you two poking around down there. It might not be safe."

"I've checked it out, Erica," said my father. "It's fine. It's probably the safest place in the house."

"It's pretty cool knowing there used to be another house there," I said.

"It's true then?" asked Mrs. Dunham.

"What's true?" I asked quickly.

"About the thirteenth-century foundations?"

"There's not much in the way of foundations left," said my father, "but there was definitely something there. The real estate agent said the last tenant did some poking around down there and was able to confirm from some wood fragments he found that it was the site of a much older building."

"Why do you suppose they took such care to preserve it when they built the next house?" asked Mrs. Dunham.

"They probably didn't," said my father. "They probably put the new house over it, and built the door and the steps leading into it so they'd have access to it for a subcellar or something."

"What's a subcellar?" I asked.

"Just a dark, cool place to store food and things they didn't want to spoil. This was well before refrigerators, remember."

"What kind of building do you think it was?" I asked.

"Probably a small cottage," he said, "lived in by someone with some connection to Dolwyddelan Castle. A peasant, probably, or a servant."

"Why do you say a connection with the castle?" I asked.

"That's the way communities were organized," he replied. "There'd be a castle, or a manor house, where the lord or prince or whoever was in charge lived. The people who lived in the town were basically allowed to be on their lord's land in exchange for farming, or serving in the military. Something like that."

"So whoever lived here worked for Prince Llywelyn ap Gruffudd?"

Mrs. Dunham gave me an astonished look.

"Where on earth did you hear that name?" she asked.

"Wasn't Dolwyddelan his castle?"

"Yes, it was," she said, "among others. His grandfather was said to have been born there, though that may just be legend."

"I'm impressed, Cris," said my father, giving me a big smile. "Where did the sudden interest in history come from? I thought the very word *medieval* made you cringe."

"I guess it's different, being in Wales and everything. We don't have seven-hundred-year-old buildings in the States."

"Well, if you're interested in Llywelyn —" began Mrs. Dunham, but she stopped when she heard a knock on the front door. She exchanged a look with my father.

"Are you expecting someone?" she asked, and he shook his head.

I got to my feet. "I'll get it," I said. "Maybe it's a package."

It was much cooler and damper in the hallway, away from the fireplace. I shivered a little as I crossed to the front door and opened it. There was a man standing there, very tall, with sandy hair mixed with gray, and deep blue eyes. He broke into a broad smile as he gave me the once-over.

"Hi there," he said.

"Hi," I replied, feeling uncomfortable.

"Is this the Dunham's? Is this where they're staying?"

"Um, yes. Can I tell them who's here?"

I heard footfalls coming down the stairs behind me, and I turned to see Miranda, still in her robe. She was looking past me at the man, her mouth wide open with astonishment. At the same time Mrs. Dunham came down the hall from the study. She took one look at the man and stopped dead in her tracks.

"Michael," she whispered.

"It's Dad! It's Daddy!" cried Miranda, and she ran to him as her mother, helpless, stared.

16

We all went into the study, where it was warm. Miranda was all over her father, but Dennis hung back. Mrs. Dunham hadn't exchanged more than a few words with her ex-husband. She sat on the big desk, next to my father, looking completely and utterly stunned.

"My God, but you're gorgeous!" Mr. Dunham said to Miranda, taking her hands in his own.

"I'm disgusting," she said, rolling her eyes. "I have a cold. I feel putrid."

"You don't look it, Randy," he said. "You're a sight for sore eyes, I'll tell you that. Hey, I've got something for you."

He reached into his pocket and pulled out a little box. Miranda opened it and squealed with delight.

"Oh, a locket! Daddy, it's beautiful! Thank you!" She threw her arms around him, and I saw Mrs. Dunham look away.

"Belated birthday present, honey. I am so sorry I couldn't make it to your party. I was all ready to go when the office called to say I had to go to London immediately. I didn't even have time to pack!"

"It's okay, Daddy," said Miranda, beaming.

I was witnessing something that really was none of my business. I knew I shouldn't be there. It was kind of weird, all of us crowded into the room. But I'd seen my father make a move to leave, and Mrs. Dunham had taken his arm and given him a pleading look, so he sat back down. As for me, I was transfixed. I felt like a deer caught in the headlights — I wanted to leave but I was totally frozen in place.

"Got something for you, too, buddy," Mr. Dunham said to Dennis. He tossed something small and red toward his son, and Dennis caught it. His eyes grew wide as he examined it, and he looked back at his father.

"A Swiss army knife," he said.

"A real one," his father said, grinning. "From Switzerland."

Dennis stared at it like it might bite him.

"I have missed you kids so much!" he said. "You can't imagine!"

"Michael, I wish you had called," Mrs. Dunham said softly.

"Oh, I wanted to call you kids so many times, so

many times! But you know how I travel, and I've been in London most of the year, and the time is all screwy here. You know, when it's noon here, it's the crack of dawn back in the States and everything."

"How did you find us?" asked Mrs. Dunham.

"Oh, well, I called the University, you know, to send you a check, and they said you were in Wales and gave me your address, and there I was in London, just a hop, skip, and a jump away . . . so . . . "

"I do wish you had called," Mrs. Dunham said.

"Mother!" said Miranda. "Just get off it! He's here now, and that's all that matters!" Her father put his arm around her.

I stared at Mrs. Dunham in surprise. What was wrong with her? Here this guy appears, out of nowhere, this guy who's attempted to kidnap their son, and yet she said nothing about it. I mean, she looked totally unhappy and stressed out, but she just stood there, allowing everything to happen. And Mr. Dunham — he was acting like everything was totally normal. Did he not think Dennis remembered somehow? Did he just expect everything to be okay?

"My little Randy," her father said. "I just can't get over how beautiful you are!"

She beamed at him. "Will you put the locket on me?" she asked, handing it to him.

"Sure, baby," he said, fastening it around her

neck. "Saw this in a shop in London, and I knew you'd just love it."

"I do," she said. "I love it."

"I found the greatest little bed-and-breakfast in town. It's just great. So cheap, you couldn't believe it."

"How long are you staying?" Miranda asked eagerly.

"I don't know, honey," he said with a grin. "How long do you want me?"

"A long time," she replied, giving her mother a look. "Maybe we could have dinner or something."

"That's a great idea!" he said. "Would you like that, Dennis? Do you want to have dinner with your old dad?"

Mrs. Dunham tensed visibly, but still she said nothing, and suddenly I realized why. As far as she knew, Dennis didn't know the real story of his father's abrupt departure. And as for Miranda, I knew if Mrs. Dunham said one hostile thing, she'd go through the roof. I could see it in the almost triumphant looks Miranda kept throwing at her mother. She was just waiting for the opportunity, and her mother didn't want to give it to her.

"Michael," Mrs. Dunham said carefully, "I think we should talk about this, before you make any plans."

"Oh, for heaven's sake, Mother," cried Miranda.

"As if you can stop us from having dinner with our own father. That is so like you!"

"Well, we do have plans to eat here tonight," my father said suddenly. "The five of us."

"The five of us?" said Mr. Dunham, staring at my father, as if seeing him for the first time. "Who are you, anyway?"

"I'm Derek Stone," my father said. "I'm doing some work of my own here, and we arranged for our families to share the house for the summer. Cristyn is my daughter," he added.

"Oh," said Mr. Dunham. Then he flashed me a smile. "How do you like Wales, honey?"

I cringed at the phoney endearment. "It's fine," I said, looking away.

"Nice country. And nice digs you got here. Very cozy."

"So yes, Daddy," said Miranda, putting her arm around his waist. "We want to have dinner with you."

"Name the day, baby," he said, rumpling her hair.

"Michael, wait," Mrs. Dunham said quickly. "I think we — can we just talk? Alone? Before you start making plans?"

"He can do anything he wants, Mother!" said Miranda. "You can't order him around anymore."

"Miranda, please, just be quiet for a moment so that we can work this out," said her mother.

"I don't want to be quiet!" Miranda shouted back.

"Okay, okay," said my father, standing up. "Look, I think everybody needs a little time to regroup here, all right? Mr. Dunham, I know you've come a long way to see your kids, but I think in fairness to everyone we should cut this visit short. Everyone needs a little time to cool down, okay?"

"Your new boyfriend's quite the diplomat," said Mr. Dunham, momentarily losing his charm.

"He's not —" Mrs. Dunham took a deep breath before continuing. "As Derek explained, we are sharing this house for the summer. Nothing more. Michael, please listen. He's right. Just let things cool down for a while. Please. Why don't you give me your phone number, and I'll call you later to discuss this. We have a lot to talk about."

"Sure, Erica," he said with a way too big smile. "Of course. I won't plan anything without checking with you first."

He pulled a piece of paper out of his pocket and rummaged around for a pen. Mrs. Dunham handed him one.

"Okay," he said scribbling. "Here's my number. You call me, Erica, whenever it's best for you, and we'll talk it over. No sweat."

He handed the paper to Mrs. Dunham, who took it silently.

"Well, I should probably skedaddle on back to my lodgings," he said.

"Dad, don't go!" cried Miranda. "She can't tell you what to do."

"It's okay, sweetheart," he said. "Your mother is absolutely right. We'll talk, and we'll make some plans. We'll have that dinner, honey, I promise."

He got up to leave, with Miranda clinging to his hand.

"Dad?" said Dennis.

"Yes, baby?" his father said, giving him another huge smile.

Dennis walked over to his father and extended his hand. He held out the Swiss army knife to his father.

"I don't want this," he said.

"Dennis, don't be such a brat!" said Miranda.

"I don't want it," he repeated.

"You're unbelievable!" cried Miranda.

"No, it's okay," said Mr. Dunham, taking the knife from his son. "He doesn't have to take it. I understand, Den."

Miranda glared at her brother, but he didn't seem to care.

"Good-bye, sweetheart," Mr. Dunham said to Miranda. "Good-bye, Denny. I'll see you guys real soon, okay?"

"I'll walk you to the door," said Miranda.

"That's okay, sweetheart, I can find my own way

out," said her father, and he walked out the door. A few seconds later, I heard the front door shut.

"I hate you," said Miranda, and she ran out of the room.

Dennis walked over to his mother, put his arms around her waist, and began to cry.

We didn't eat dinner at all that night.

17

I felt Miranda glaring at me as I got ready for bed.

"What?" I said.

"Just don't say it," she said, dabbing furiously at her nose with a tissue.

"Don't say what?" I asked.

"You know exactly what I mean," she said. "You're on his side now. Just like my mother. Everyone goes over to Dennis's side eventually. I just don't want to hear any self-righteous crap from you. You don't know anything about this."

At some point in my life I realized that I had inherited my father's gift for peacemaking. I just hadn't developed that amazing knack he had to use it, instead of throwing a fit. I knew, though, that this was the time to end the war, no matter how unpleasant a task. I took a deep breath.

"Miranda," I said, "I'm not on anybody's side, okay?"

"Bull!" she cried. "You've been buddy-buddy with the little twerp for the last two days!"

"That's true," I said. "I have been hanging out with Dennis. I like him, Miranda. I do."

She made an exasperated noise and rolled her eyes.

"But, Miranda, this isn't a one or the other deal here. Just because I'm getting along with Dennis doesn't mean I've taken a side against you."

"You said you hated me," she said, sniffling.

"I know. I'm sorry. I just — I barely know you and suddenly you're fighting with me like I'm your sister, or something. I just needed a break, okay?"

"Yeah, well, I'm sorry I'm such a disaster that you need a vacation from me."

I took another deep breath.

"Miranda, we haven't even been here for two weeks. Let's just work our stuff out, okay? We were having a good time there for a while, right?"

"You sound like your father," she said, and I laughed.

"Thanks," I said.

"I just felt so awful when you went off with Dennis like that, and then I had to go and get sick, and now Dad shows up and Mother's being such a monster . . ."

Tears started rolling down her face. Boy, can this girl cry. I sat next to her on the bed and put my arm around her.

"She doesn't understand," she wept, "that just because she doesn't love him anymore doesn't mean I don't!"

"She wants you to love him, Miranda," I said. "I know she does."

"She doesn't!" she said. "You heard her. She doesn't even want me to have one lousy dinner with him!"

I knew why Mrs. Dunham was afraid to leave Miranda alone with her father, but there was no way I could explain that to her without breaking Mrs. Dunham's confidence.

"I just really think she does understand that, Miranda."

"Well, we'll see. We'll just see about that," she sniffed, rubbing at her wet, red eyes.

"Yeah, okay," I said. "Can I see your locket?"

She brightened a little and pulled it out from inside her nightgown. It was a little oval locket, gold-colored, but I could tell it wasn't real. Actually, it looked kind of cheap, but this probably wasn't a good day to start a career as a jewelry appraiser.

"It's really pretty," I said.

"Isn't it?" she asked. "My mother never gives me anything."

Except food, shelter, clothes, and the occasional trip to Wales. But why mess up a good thing?

"It's really nice, Miranda," I repeated, and this time I was rewarded with a smile.

"Thanks," she said. "I am sorry, and stuff. I shouldn't have said that thing, about wishing my mother was dead. I didn't mean it like that — I just wasn't thinking. I forgot."

"But you should think," I said, "I mean, you should know. That's a rotten thing to wish. You don't want that wish to come true."

"I didn't mean it," she sniffed. "I'm sorry. I am, okay?"

"Done," I said. "Hatchet buried."

"Really?" she said, looking surprised.

"Really."

"Okay," she said, still sniffling. "So, um, did you go down? To the cellar?"

"Yeah," I said.

"And? Anything happen?"

"Something. I think. It's kind of a long story. Can I tell you tomorrow?"

"Definitely," she said, pulling the covers up to her chin.

"Okay. Good night."

"Good night, Cris."

I was truly exhausted when I crawled into bed. I felt like I'd spent an entire day running a nursery school. I fell asleep while wondering if anyone else's father was going to pop out of the woodwork tomorrow.

18

The next morning, Mrs. Dunham sur-prised everybody by suggesting that we invite Mr. Dunham over to dinner that evening.

"Here? Why?" asked Miranda, staring at her mother from the opposite side of the kitchen.

"Isn't that what you want? Don't you want to have dinner with him?" her mother asked, casting a glance over at Dennis, who was tinkering with the wood-burning stove.

"I don't know," Miranda said a little sullenly.

"I talked to him a little while ago, on the phone, and he said he'd like to do that. To have dinner with all of us."

"Well no one asked me what I'd like," Miranda said, opening and closing the refrigerator door.

"I am asking you, sweetheart. I'm asking you

now. Would you like to have your father over to dinner tonight?"

"Where will you be?" she asked.

"Here, with you," she said. "We'll have a feast. Cristyn's father is quite the amateur chef, I'm told. So what do you think, honey?"

Miranda shrugged and closed the refrigerator door with her knee.

"I don't know," she said. "I guess. Whatever."

"Great," said her mother. "Would you like to call him?"

"You're letting me call him, now?" Miranda said with a little scowl.

"The number is in the study by the phone," Mrs. Dunham said. "I'm sure he'd really like the official invitation to come from you."

"Okay," Miranda said suddenly, darting out of the room.

"Dennis," said Mrs. Dunham. "Is this okay with you?"

Dennis looked thoughtful, then glanced over at me.

"Will Cristyn be there?" he asked, and I nodded.

"Okay," he said and turned back to the stove. I felt sorry for him, looking at his little hunched shoulders from behind. Nobody thinks he knows what's going on, I thought. They think he's too little. But I knew Dennis was aware of exactly what was going on. And I don't think he liked it at all.

"Maybe we should just start eating," said my father, looking around at all of us. We had been sitting around the kitchen table, pretty much in silence, for what seemed like a really long time.

"We can put his plate on the stove, to keep the food warm," my father added.

"He isn't coming," said Dennis.

"Shut up, Dennis!" cried Miranda. "He is coming!"

"He isn't coming," Dennis repeated softly.

I had to agree. We'd been waiting for over two hours, first in the study, watching the cheese Mrs. Dunham had set out grow all soft and gooey. And now in the kitchen, where Mr. Dunham's empty place spoke for itself.

"What did you do?" Miranda said suddenly to her mother. "What did you say to him?"

"I didn't do anything, Miranda," she said. "You spoke to him last. Are you sure you told him six o'clock?"

"You must have done something!" she cried. "You must have said something. You didn't want him here in the first place."

"Miranda, it was my idea!" she said. "Why would I —"

"This is exactly what you wanted to happen, isn't it! You wanted him to look bad — you wanted to prove something!"

"That isn't true, Miranda!" Mrs. Dunham tried. "Do you think I wanted to see you hurt again? That's the last thing I wanted!"

"Then why isn't he here?"

Mrs. Dunham took a deep breath.

"I don't know. I honestly don't. Do you want to call him? Would that make you feel better?"

"No. I don't know. Maybe."

"The number is still by the phone in the study."

Miranda looked at her mother suddenly, like a kind of plea.

"What do I say?" she asked, her voice shaking a little.

"Just . . . " Mrs. Dunham sighed. "Just let him know you were worried about him. Ask if everything is all right."

"Okay," said Miranda, getting up from her chair.

"Do you want me to come?" called Dennis, but she was already out the door.

After a moment, my dad got up and started serving the food. Poor Dad, I thought, staring at the roast chicken he'd worked so hard over. I wasn't the only one getting more than I'd bargained for. We ate in silence for a few minutes.

"Are you okay?" my father asked Mrs. Dunham.

"I don't know," she said, poking at the chicken with her fork. "I feel so stupid. I really thought we might be able to have a nice evening together. But Michael hasn't changed," she added, casting a glance over at Dennis.

"Well, maybe something came up," my father began, but Mrs. Dunham shook her head.

"No, I don't think so. I should have realized something like this would happen. I should have let them go somewhere alone, with him. He just — he wants to be a father to them when he feels like it. On his own terms. I shouldn't have tried to get him to come here. I just felt safer — I mean, I just wanted to be there. God, I've made such a mess out of it!"

"You didn't make a mess, Mom," said Dennis quietly. "Daddy just is that way."

He turned his attention back to his dinner as his mother looked at him in surprise. Maybe she'll realize now how smart he is, I thought, watching him eat with a serious look on his face. Maybe she'll realize that he knows more than anyone thinks he does.

Miranda suddenly appeared in the doorway.

"Nobody answered," she said, sitting back down at the table.

Nobody really said much after that. I sat staring at the door to the cellar, thinking about Carwen.

Missing her. What would Carwen think of this dysfunctional scene? Perhaps we'd scared her off. She might have decided we were the wrong people to help her. Maybe she was never coming back. I would have to go back down after her, then. I needed Carwen back. I had to know what was happening to her, and what she wanted of me. She needed help. Come to think of it, so did everyone in the house.

A few hours after lunch the next day, Miranda set off into the hills by herself. Dennis stayed up in his room and wouldn't come out. Mrs. Dunham looked like she was about to have a complete nervous breakdown, and Dad didn't say much of anything to anyone, though he looked kind of sad.

I sat in the kitchen near the wood-burning stove, reading and tinkering with the idea of going into the basement alone. Surprise of surprises, it had been drizzling on and off for most of the day, so once again, I couldn't go down to the stone circle as I wanted to. Just when I thought it might be best for everyone involved if I simply lay down and died of boredom, my father appeared briefly in the kitchen and told me he thought it would be okay if I telephoned Charlotte. It was 3:30 Welsh time, which would be 9:30 in the morning for Charlotte. Late enough to call. I'd already agreed there would be no transatlantic gossip calls, but I wasn't going to argue with my father's sudden change of heart.

Charlotte didn't sound like she was on the other side of the ocean. She sounded close. Real close. I could even hazard a guess as to what kind of gum she was chewing.

"This is too totally weird," said Charlotte. "I was just, this very second, wishing I could tell you."

"Tell me what?" I asked, getting into the yakking-with-Charlotte position on my father's bed, feet waving in the air.

"Okay, A, or one, or whatever, Geoff's big brother went out and got so totally drunk that the police came and took him home, and they made Geoff, like, sign for him before they'd leave."

"All right, so we have a heavy drinker in the family. Next?"

"Okay, B, or —"

"Two," I prompted.

". . . right, is that finally, after dreaming about it for, like, two years, Dina got her picture taken with Regis and Kathie Lee."

"Excellent," I said.

"And she's going to use it for a Christmas card."

"I should hope."

"Right. So then, also, Christine and Suzanne got into this major fight in the middle of the mall, and

Christine blew her beanie in a big way and said something so radically rude that Suzanne ended up slapping her. On the face. And I am dead serious on that. It, like, left a *mark*."

These blessed moments of being back in her world sent my spirits soaring. Charlotte Hospital. As the Charlotte Turns. The Young and the Charlotte. I could have spent the whole summer like this, a relaxed and friendly observer of the frenzied, nonstop drama that was Charlotte Hawthorne. How could the worlds of Miranda Dunham and Charlotte Hawthorne exist side by side? And what would happen if they touched? Surely the universe as we know it would come to a swift and utter end.

"What?"

"You heard me. What's the professor like? Is her daughter a cow, or can't you talk? Is she in the room? Should we go to code?"

"She's not even in the house, Char. She's out walking."

"Details," Charlotte demanded.

"I don't know," I said. "She's all right. She's not — she's just kind of difficult, I guess."

"Difficult?"

"Yeah. Moody, mostly. I mean, at first it seemed like it would work out pretty well and all, but she keeps wigging out on me. She's mad at her brother, she's mad at her mother, and if I so much as look at either of them, she gets mad at me, too."

"Sounds like terminal PMS," said Charlotte thoughtfully.

"No, I mean, she's had some problems and everything, like with her father blowing town, and stuff, so I can't really blame her."

"So you hate her?" Charlotte asked kind of hopefully.

"Not really, no. And sometimes I really like her. When she's not throwing a fit at someone, that is. It's going to be a long summer if we can't work something out. But we're speaking again, so we'll see."

"You weren't speaking?" said Charlotte.

"For a little while."

"A little while? You've been there, like, two weeks."

"I know. Anyway, it'll be okay. I don't really want to talk about it anymore. I'm sick of it, you know?"

"Exactly," Charlotte said emphatically. "I cannot tell you how many times Christine has called me to discuss the fact that she has this red blotch in the shape of three of Suzanne's fingers on her cheek. Her life is like this huge soap opera I'm addicted to."

"I know the feeling," I said, but I held the receiver away from my mouth when I said it.

"So what else is happening?" Charlotte prompted.

"Nothing," I said.

"Has your dad hooked up with the professor lady?"

"What is with everybody on that subject!" I said. "They barely know each other. Get real, Charlotte."

"Well," she said, sounding a little hurt, "then, what else?"

I sighed. "I'm being haunted."

"What?"

"I'm being haunted."

"Haunted."

"Haunted. By the ghost of a teenage girl who lived on this spot in the thirteenth century, when Llywelyn ap Gruffudd was trying to save Wales from the English. She lives in this cottage and she waits for her father every day and now he's come but she wants something and I don't know what because she doesn't speak to me and when she does speak it's in Welsh." As I took a deep breath to re-place all the air I'd just squeezed from my lungs in forming that amazing sentence, there was silence from the other end of the line. A long silence. Finally, Charlotte began to laugh hysterically.

"You are too funny," she said between giggles. "You actually had me going there for a minute."

Okay. Thinking I could tell Charlotte was

officially a Really Dumb Idea. Carefully, I steered the conversation back to Christine's complexion, away from Wales, away from Miranda, and away from Carwen who even now might be waiting for me to come back to her.

19

Dennis still wouldn't come out of his room. I knocked on his door a couple of times, but he didn't answer, so I respected his privacy and let him alone. Although it was almost seven o'clock, Miranda still hadn't returned from her walk. My father had gone out looking for her, but with no success. The tense feeling hanging over the house was almost unbearable. I argued with myself back and forth, toying with the idea, and finally decided to go down into the cellar alone. True, it was getting dark, but the cellar was always pitch-black anyway, so was it really any creepier to go at night?

I put on a heavy sweater and a pair of comfortable sneakers, and retrieved the flashlight from where Dennis had left it in the kitchen. I hesitated at the oak door, then swallowed my fears and slid the lock back. I was already looking around in anticipation before I was even halfway down the steps, so I guess

I shouldn't have been surprised when I slipped and rolled heavily down to the dirt floor. The flashlight, Old Reliable, blinked helpfully off. I lay, momentarily stunned, in a little heap at the bottom of the stairs. Taking inventory, I was almost annoyed to discover that I didn't seem to be hurt at all. You'd think after tumbling down ten stone steps there'd at least be a fracture or something, but I seemed to be all in one piece. I stood up and brushed myself off. Then I sensed movement, and looked up to see not one but three figures standing under the stairs. Carwen was there, and her father, and a third. She was a very pretty woman, wearing a long, elegant dress of brightly colored fabric. She had a kind of headdress of fabric framing her face, making her look almost nunlike, but something in it looked familiar, and I knew it must be a fashion of the times. Definitely an important lady, I thought. I could also not help but notice that she was extremely pregnant. Carwen's father was gesturing toward her, and it seemed as if he was indicating that she should wait. She didn't look happy.

Carwen's father was speaking to her in low, urgent tones. Carwen was listening intently and periodically nodding at something her father said. I got the feeling he was giving her instructions, or something. As he spoke to his daughter, the older woman looked about nervously. She seemed anxious, and I wondered how far she'd have to travel in her hugely pregnant state. She approached him and gently took his arm in her hand.

"Llywelyn," she said softly.

Carwen's father was Llywelyn! That explained a lot. But what was the daughter of such a great Welsh prince doing living in a tiny cottage, wearing an old dress and going barefoot?

Llywelyn turned briefly to the woman and said something that seemed reassuring. She must be his wife, I thought. But I got the distinct feeling that she wasn't Carwen's mother.

Llywelyn reached into the folds of his cloak and pulled out something small and glittering. Carwen's eyes widened as he reached around her and fastened the necklace around her throat. She reached one hand up to clasp the pendant, and reached for her father with her other hand. He embraced her for a long time, then finally stepped back. This clearly wasn't a casual good-bye. There was something very final, and very sad, in the expressions of father and daughter as they exchanged a look. Llywelyn took his wife's hand in his own and called her something that might have been Ellen or Eleanor. She embraced Carwen briefly, then she and Llywelyn turned toward me and began to walk away. Just before the picture blinked off, two images set in my mind. The first was Carwen, her hand clutching the necklace at her throat, her expression unreadable. The second was an image of Llywelyn himself, because he was no longer dressed in the same way I'd seen him previously. I'm no expert on the fashion trends of the medieval Welsh, but Llywelyn was unmistakably dressed for battle. Wales was at war.

Mrs. Dunham was sitting at the kitchen table, staring into a cup of tea, when I appeared. She gave a great shriek when I opened the door, and a little wave of steaming tea spilled onto the table.

"Sorry," I said sheepishly, retrieving a dish towel to mop up the mess. "I didn't mean to frighten you."

"What were you doing?" she asked. "You're covered in dirt. Are you all right?"

"I'm fine. I was just doing a little exploring. Junior archaeologist and all that."

Maybe it was the strain of the day's events that had gotten to her, but Mrs. Dunham didn't seem to find it at all strange that I'd been poking around in the cellar in the middle of the night. She just nodded and stared back at the tea.

"Um, did Miranda . . ."

"Upstairs," Mrs. Dunham replied, and I nodded, relieved. "I was on the verge of calling the police.

But apparently she just wanted to spend some time by herself."

"Is everything okay then?" I asked.

"No," she replied. "But it's out of my hands now, I'm afraid." She sighed and cupped her hands around her mug of tea, shivering slightly.

"Mrs. Dunham?" I asked, inwardly questioning my timing. She looked up at me expectantly. "Would you tell me about Llywelyn?"

For a minute, I thought she had no idea what I was talking about, but then she said, "Llywelyn ap Gruffudd? The one you mentioned the other day?"

I nodded. "What does *ap* mean, anyway?"

"Son of," she said. "Like Mac. His father's name was Gruffudd."

"Can you tell me about him?" I asked. If she thought my request was strange, she didn't say so. Maybe the prince was a welcome diversion after the events of the last two days.

"It's funny you should hone in on him," she said. "Of all the figures in history, he's one of my favorites. Let's see. Llywelyn came to power in Wales sometime around 1250. Wales had been divided into a number of little kingdoms, and they always fought against each other. He managed to unite most of his country against King Edward and the English, but as you might have guessed, he lost in the end. I'll tell you, though, his life was something right out of the storybooks."

"Why?" I asked.

"Well, he'd been engaged to Elinor de Montfort, who was the daughter of Simon de Montfort. Do you know who he is?" I shook my head. "He's another story. But he was a very powerful English lord who rebelled against the English crown and was eventually killed. After that, the marriage plans between Llywelyn and Simon de Montfort's daughter were canceled, but for some reason years later Llywelyn decided that he still wanted to marry her. She was rumored to be very beautiful, and she came from a great family, and King Edward was furious when he heard that they'd married by proxy."

"Why? What's marriage by proxy?"

"They each took their vows separately, from their own countries. Elinor was living in France at the time. Edward thought it was pretty rotten of this rebellious Welsh prince to marry the daughter of a man who'd rebelled against him. And to make things really confusing, Elinor was Edward's cousin. It was a match that was bound to cause him trouble. So when Elinor sailed to Wales intending to join her new husband, Edward kidnapped her."

"No way!" I said.

"Yep. He kept her confined for almost three years and used her as a bargaining chip to help end the war Llywelyn was waging against the English crown."

"That's terrible!" I said, thinking of Llywelyn's sad, lined face. "Did he ever get her back?"

"Eventually," she said, smiling. "In around 1278. But they didn't have much time together. Elinor died bearing their first child, in the summer of 1282."

"Twelve eighty-two?"

"Uh-huh. Twelve eighty-two was a bad year for the Welsh."

"What happened then?"

"Llywelyn's youngest brother, Dafydd, had started up the rebellion again on his own. They'd been at odds with each other in the past, but with Elinor dead, and their only child a girl, Llywelyn had lost all hope of producing a male heir. So he joined with Dafydd."

"But they didn't win?"

"Things were going okay for a while, but then Llywelyn rode down south to a place called Builth, where he was trying to get more support for the rebellion. What happened then is pretty much of a mystery."

"Why?"

"One night in late December, something made him leave his stronghold. There are different theories as to what it was, but whatever happened,

Llywelyn was out riding with only a small number of armed men. They encountered some English soldiers and fought with them. One of the soldiers, not realizing who he was fighting, killed Llywelyn. After he'd killed him, someone recognized him, and they cut off his head and brought it back to Edward, who was greatly pleased."

"What happened to the brother? Dafydd?"

"Some months later he was hunted down and executed. And that was more or less the end of the Welsh rebellion. Edward wanted to make very sure that Wales would never threaten him again, so he built these immense castles all through the country and filled them with his soldiers. After that, there was just no hope. It wasn't until Owain Glyndwyr came along over 100 years later that another major rebellion was born. But that one failed, too, in the end. There's an article about Llywelyn in one of my periodicals. I can lend it to you if you like."

I thought back to what I'd just seen in the cellar. Llywelyn's wife had been very pregnant. She had no idea, I thought, that she wouldn't live another month. But if they'd only been married for a few years, then who was Carwen?

"Was Llywelyn ever married to anyone else?" I asked, and Mrs. Dunham shook her head. "So he had no other children?"

"He certainly didn't have any sons," she said. "Illegitimacy wasn't necessarily viewed as an obstacle, and we know Llywelyn rested all his hopes on Elinor to produce an heir. But I suppose it's possible he may have had a daughter. Remember, he didn't marry Elinor until he was in his late forties, so there had certainly been other women in his life."

"What would he have done with an illegitimate daughter if he'd had one?" I asked.

"Hard to say. Different men dealt with it in different ways. Sometimes the child would be brought up in the court, or kept somewhere close and provided for. Sometimes the child was abandoned altogether. Or sent to a convent. Llywelyn and Elinor's daughter was sent to a convent when he was killed. She lived there all her life. I wonder about her sometimes, whether she knew who her father was, and what he'd stood for. What he'd accomplished."

"Was Wales at war when Elinor died?"

"Yes."

Then from the moment I'd seen him tonight, all was lost for Llywelyn. Perhaps he'd been making a last, desperate effort to provide for Carwen somehow before going off to fight. But I knew now that shortly Elinor and Llywelyn were both to die, and something was going to happen to Carwen. Something bad enough for her to still be seeking to change it, after seven hundred years.

"That's so sad," I said, feeling helpless.

"It's the saddest thing in the world for a child to not know a father," Mrs. Dunham replied, and I knew she was talking about something else, something far removed from the doomed Welsh prince and the daughter he loved but could not protect.

I couldn't escape from Carwen and Llywelyn, not even in sleep. The dream started the same way, with Carwen leaping onto the horse, her face full of fear. She clung to the horse as it reared, urging it forward with sharp cries. And again, I became aware of a sound in the background, a sharp, crackling sound. This time I knew what it was. Carwen's cottage was on fire, and its red glow engulfed her as she tried to make her escape.

20

On Tuesday, two days after our attempted dinner, Mr. Dunham finally called. I gathered from what I heard that he was claiming he had a stomach virus, or something. Whatever the story was, Miranda seemed to buy it, or pretended she did. He offered to make up for his "illness" by taking Miranda and Dennis out to lunch in town. Mrs. Dunham agreed, which seemed to take Miranda a little by surprise. Dennis, not surprisingly, said he didn't want to go.

Miranda's father picked her up at about one o'clock. He didn't even get out of the car, just honked once. Miranda ran straight out and climbed into the car. I watched as they pulled away down the driveway. Dad and Mrs. Dunham had both gone to the library, and Dennis was nowhere to be seen. He was probably still in his room. I'd tried to talk to him again that morning, but he'd said he really didn't feel like talking. In truth, though, I think it was Miranda he wanted.

I went upstairs to my room and settled onto my bed with a book, but I couldn't concentrate. The house was absolutely silent, and it felt as if I was the only person in it. I stared up at the wooden beams in the ceiling, listening for something, any clue that I wasn't alone.

"Carwen," I called softly, once, but if she heard me, she gave no indication of it. Whatever it was she wanted me to discover about her, she wanted to show me on her own terms, not mine.

I sat up in bed suddenly and stared at my mother's picture. It was her engagement picture, taken when she was probably in her early twenties. She was beautiful, I thought, though the black-and-white picture gave no hint of the amazing color of her hair. And I realized something as I looked at that picture. I looked like my mother. Not that I'm beautiful. And my hair isn't red; it's more of an auburn. But the resemblance was there. We looked alike.

I don't know why I told people I didn't miss her, why I said it was no big deal when they asked. It was a big deal. It seemed the older I got, the more I missed her. Most of my friends complained ceaselessly about their mothers, how they wouldn't let them wear makeup, or stay out late, and how they nagged and criticized. I usually sympathized with them and agreed when they said I was lucky not to have to deal with all that, but I didn't mean it. I would have accepted all of her motherly pressures gladly, and then some, just to have her there. With me.

Sometimes I wondered where she was. Dad wasn't much into the church thing, except on Christmas, and that was okay with me. But sometimes I thought about going, just to see if I might find an answer there, about where she was or something. I knew enough about God to know my mother was supposed to be in heaven, but nobody actually seems to know what that means. They say it to you like it's a big comforting thing that should make you feel better, but they never tell you where it is, or how to get there, or whether you can talk to somebody who's already there.

Carwen was dead, and yet I could see her. But what was I really seeing? Was I really encountering the living Carwen? All I had really experienced was some noises, some furniture moving around, and a kind of miniseries down in the basement that seemed to tell a story. But was that really Carwen, or had whatever happened to her been so powerful that it just kept replaying itself? Maybe those scenes in the cellar went on all the time, whether I was there or not. Of the living, feeling Carwen

I had experienced nothing. It didn't seem she could see me at all, down in the cellar. I watched things happen to her, but it was as if I wasn't even there.

I think that's what bothered me most about my mother being dead. That she didn't know me. That I had a life, that I looked like her, and was growing up and turning into this person and was possibly even on the brink of getting a boyfriend, and she had no idea. If Carwen could contact me, and move things around, and show me things, why couldn't my mother? Why wouldn't she?

Frustrated, I lay back on the bed and opened my book. I stared at the words for a long time before I finally noticed what they said and began to make sense of them.

"The food was awful," said Miranda, looking more animated than she had in days, "but I didn't care. It was so cool being with my dad again, you just can't imagine."

It hadn't actually begun to rain yet, but the sky was heavy with dark clouds, so it was only a matter of time.

"Well, it's good that you had fun, and everything," I said, staring up at the sky. I hadn't wanted to share the stone circle with Miranda, so we lounged instead on some weak-looking lawn chairs that my father had discovered and placed behind the house.

"It was excellent!" she said. "I can't even begin to tell you. So what have you been doing all day?"

I'd been feeling really depressed since I'd spoken with Mrs. Dunham last night after I'd seen Carwen, and thinking about my mother that afternoon had just made things worse. The burden of knowing Llywelyn's and Carwen's future was weighing really heavily on me. It was so sad, so hopeless. Why was she showing me these last moments of her life? They were her last moments, somehow I was sure of that. With Elinor and Llywelyn dead, and King Edward's soldiers tearing up the countryside, there was no hope for my Carwen, alone and un-protected in her cottage.

"God, Cristyn, what's wrong? Did something happen?"

I nodded as tears spilled out onto my cheeks. I felt such sadness, and I wasn't sure where it was coming from. My mother's face was so clear in my mind, but I refused to believe she was causing this mood. She was nowhere, she was gone. It was Carwen who wouldn't leave my thoughts. Carwen who wanted me, who asked something of me, who needed me.

"I am such a cow!" exclaimed Miranda, scram-bling to my side and placing a hand on my arm.

"Here I am babbling about my stupid lunch, and I never even asked . . . is it your dad? Did something happen?"

I shook my head and looked into her face.

"It's Carwen," I mumbled.

"Carwen?"

"She's the — I've been going down into the cellar. With Dennis, except last night I was alone. She's the one, Miranda. Her name is Carwen, and she's our age, and she lived here. The Prince Llywelyn that we read about was her father, but she was illegitimate, and he kept her here and tried to take care of her."

"Wo, wo, wait a second. You're talking, like, a ghost? You've actually seen her?"

"Dennis said that she wanted me. He saw her, Miranda, before. He'd seen her all along. So we went down there, where he said she was, and it was like these scenes started playing back, like a movie or something."

"Wait, wait, wait. What did you see? What happened?"

I sighed and recounted every detail of what I'd seen. When I finished, Miranda sat for a long time without saying anything.

"This is . . . too weird. Cris I swear, if you are making this up —"

"I'm not!" I said sharply. "If you're scared, then fine. We don't have to talk about it."

"I'm not scared!" she said. "I just . . . you have to admit, Cris, it's pretty hard to believe. But I do believe you," she added quickly. "I do. I just . . . I wish I'd been there, that's all. Why didn't you tell me?"

"You were sick, you were mad. We were fighting, remember? And then your father showed up, and things got . . . well, you know. I don't know. I didn't think you cared, really."

"Well, God, I'd think you could have at least . . . well, maybe not. Okay. So explain it again, though. What's so terrible?"

"I told you, last night, I saw her father come to her, with his wife. He was trying to tell Carwen something, and he looked so sad. And he gave her something. A necklace. And then he left. He was dressed like he was going to battle, and he looked so sad."

"What does it mean?"

"I don't know. I talked to your mom, last night, and she told me all about Llywelyn. When I saw his wife, she looked really pregnant, like it was almost time, and your mother said that she died giving birth to that child. Things were getting really serious with this whole rebellion he had going against the English, and a few months after his wife died, he got killed."

"But that doesn't mean Carwen won't be okay," said Miranda.

"It does, somehow. Your mother said after Llywelyn was killed, King Edward sent soldiers into Wales to crush any resistance and make the people afraid to do anything. Something bad is going to happen to Carwen, I just know it."

"Not necessarily," said Miranda.

"Yes, necessarily," I said. "There's something else, too. I keep having this dream about her. I've been having it since the first day I got here, actually, but I just hadn't put two and two together. In this dream, the cottage is on fire and she's really scared, and she's trying to get away. But somehow, I don't think she does."

"Maybe there's something about her in the encyclopedia, or in one of the history books."

"I don't think so," I said. "If she was an illegitimate daughter and everything, I don't think she'd be given any big place in the history books or anything."

"You don't know that," said Miranda, getting to her feet. "We can look, anyway. There's like twelve different Welsh history books in the study. I'll just grab a couple. We can check, okay?"

"Okay," I said, and Miranda walked down the

path that led to the front door. It felt good to tell her about Carwen. Dennis was wonderful, but I couldn't confide to him what I feared was happening and how desperately sad and afraid I was for Carwen. Maybe he knew what was happening anyway. But I just couldn't talk to him the way I could to Miranda.

I tried again to piece everything together in my mind. With Elinor and Llywelyn dead, and the English clamping down violently throughout the country, all of Wales would be in shambles. There would be nowhere for Carwen to turn. Anyone her father might have known and trusted, anyone who might have been a help to her, would have been on the top of Edward's list to knock off. Her only hope would be to stay quiet, and try not to call attention to herself, or to flee. But something had happened. The cottage was on fire — could Edward's soldiers have been attacking the town? Mrs. Dunham had said that Dolwyddelan was one of Llywelyn's castles. Could Edward have attacked it and burned the town to make sure no one would be able to organize another rebellion in Llywelyn's name?

I was so deep in thought I didn't notice Miranda had returned until she was right in front of me. I looked up at her expectantly, but she didn't have any books. Her face was unnaturally white.

"Where are the books?" I asked. "What's wrong?"

"I went to the study," she said, not meeting my eye.

"Where are the books?" I repeated.

"My mom and your dad. They didn't see me, but I saw them. They were together. Cristyn, they were kissing."

21

For a while, we both pretended like it just hadn't happened. At dinner that night they acted just like they always had, joking around and getting lost in talk about medieval stuff that we couldn't follow at all. Neither Miranda nor I said much, and I felt my father looking at me occasionally, but I pretended I didn't notice.

The next day, though, they emerged unexpectedly from the study and announced we were all going to lunch at this pub they'd heard about, called the Ty Gwyn.

I went upstairs to get a sweater, and Miranda followed me.

"You should bring something warm," I said, but she shook her head.

"I'm not going," she said.

"Oh, come on, Miranda, you've got to go!"

"No way," she said.

"Miranda, please," I said softly. "After what hap-pened — I'd just really like you to be there. With me."

"Dennis will be there," she said.

"That's not the same, and you know it. Come on. Please?"

She shrugged and looked at the floor.

"Think of all the sheep you'll miss!" I said, nudg-ing her. "All those sheep you've never seen before, standing, eating, making strange noises. You can't possibly pass up an opportunity like that! Please, Miranda," I added. "I really need you to go with me."

She started to smile a little bit and nodded.

"Okay," she said. "Since you're begging, and everything."

"I'm not begging!" I said, pulling a sweater over my head.

"Pleading, then," she said, still smiling.

"Pleading I can live with," I said. "Hey, Miranda? There's one other thing. Could you — I mean, could you maybe be a little nicer to Dennis?"

"Oh, here we go," she said, rolling her eyes. "My mother has finally lured you over to her side."

"Stop it with the sides! I'm not saying it for her, I'm saying it for me. I like him, Miranda, I do. He's sweet. He really really misses you."

"How can he miss me when I'm right here?" she asked, not meeting my eye.

"You know what I mean."

"He's asked for it," she said. "You can't deny he's been a little brat."

"He's eight years old, Miranda! It's his job to be a brat. It's, like, required!"

"That doesn't mean I have to like it."

"If you could just, you know, not —"

"Fine. Okay. Agreed. Just stop the lecturing. I have one mother, and that's enough. Oh, God, I'm sorry, that didn't come out right." She looked anxiously at me.

"It's okay," I said. "I know what you meant. Let's go. I'm really hungry."

"Don't get your hopes up," she said, following me out the door. "These Welsh people could seriously use some cooking lessons from your dad."

The Ty Gwyn was another really old building, with low ceilings and thick, dark rafters. It didn't seem like anything in Wales had been built less than two hundred years ago. I kind of liked that about it. Like some things could go on and on, without changing.

We sat around a large wooden table, close enough to the fireplace to help take the chill out of my bones. I noticed my father held Erica's chair out for her as she sat down. I couldn't remember if he'd always done that, or if it was something new. A young woman came to our table and took our orders for sodas, writing it all down on her pad with a slight frown, like we'd asked for something unusual and exotic. We were alone in the room except for one other table right by the fireplace, where an old man kept repeating to his companion, "All I want is some service. I've paid for it, and I want it. Am I right? Am I right?"

"Mr. Stone," whispered Dennis loudly. "What is wrong with that man?"

"He wants service, I guess," said my father.

"He's paid for it, and he wants it," I added.

"What's service?" asked Dennis.

"Not this," said Miranda, looking around for the waitress, who was nowhere to be seen.

"Miranda," said Mrs. Dunham, "I never got to hear about your lunch yesterday. Did you — was it fun?"

Miranda looked kind of sharply at her mother, and I hoped she wasn't about to fly off the handle again. But she seemed to think the better of it and gave one of her trademark shrugs.

"Yeah, it was fine. It was great, that is. Really good. Except, you know, he couldn't eat that much. Because of his stomach, and everything."

"Where did you go?" asked my father, looking around for the waitress.

"Oh, this pub, or whatever you call them. It was called the Crossed Wires, or the Crossed Keys, or something like that. Yeah, we had a great time. And then we walked through town and went to stores and stuff. He bought me a Wales T-shirt. He bought one for you, too, Dennis."

"Thank you," Dennis said, to no one in particular.

"But he had to go back into London for a few days, he said. I think he said a few days. So he's going to call. When he gets back."

"Can we —" began Mrs. Dunham, squirming around in her chair to get a better view of the place. "Is she coming back? Should someone go after her?"

"What's the rush?" asked Miranda. "What's the big deal? She'll get here when she gets here."

"You're right," said Mrs. Dunham, settling back in her chair. She was trying, I had to give her that.

"Besides, isn't the whole point of this family time or something?" asked Miranda.

"Sure," said Mrs. Dunham quickly. "Exactly."

"Then we must be in therapy heaven," Miranda responded, looking around. "Trapped in a deserted restaurant, all facing each other. Dr. . . . what's her name . . . Dr. Joyce Brothers would be proud."

Was it my imagination, or was Miranda's icy attitude toward her mother melting slightly?

"Miranda and I want to know what the sheep think about all day," I said.

"I don't think sheep have the same, shall we say, mental requirements that humans do," said my father, grinning. "How many sheep do you know that watch television?"

"I bet they'd watch it if they could," said Miranda. "I bet they'd like TV a lot better than staring at grass all day."

"Maybe it takes a higher life form to get enjoyment without man-made diversions," said Mrs. Dunham. "Maybe sheep have a really beautiful existence because they do absolutely nothing, all the time."

"Then maybe our waitress is really a sheep," stated Dennis, and everybody laughed, even Miranda.

"I don't know," my father said. "We know she's doing absolutely nothing, but is she enjoying herself?"

"Let's all bleat, and see if that gets her attention," I said, and Dennis started right in on a high pitched baa-ing sound.

"Dennis, stop it," his mother whispered, but when the waitress actually appeared, seconds later, we all dissolved into peals of laughter. She distributed our drinks, and put down a pile of menus on our table, departing without a word.

"We're going to be here all day," said Miranda, getting up. "Cris, I'm going to find the bathroom. Want to come?"

I nodded and stood up. We looked around, then set off past the man still muttering about service, through a doorway that looked promising. Instead of a bathroom, though, we found ourselves in a little lounge, with another fireplace.

"They sure have a lot of fireplaces in this country," I said, moving toward it.

"Good thing," said Miranda, joining me.

"So, this isn't so bad, right?" I asked.

"Whatever," she said. "Yeah. It's not so bad."

"So what do you think?"

"About what?" she asked, holding her hands out toward the fire.

"About what? About them! Dad and your mom. They don't seem any different. I mean, do they? To you?"

"I don't know," she said, rubbing her hands together. "I've been thinking about it, Cris. Maybe I was wrong."

"Wrong?"

"Maybe I was wrong about . . . what I saw."

I turned to face her. "Miranda, you said they were kissing."

"I know."

"How can you be wrong about a kiss? Either it was a kiss, or it wasn't. Which was it?"

She sighed. "It was. Kind of."

"Miranda, there's no such thing as a 'kind of' kiss."

"Sure there is," she said. "I mean, oh, God, this is so embarrassing. . . . I just saw them for a split second, you know? And it was, oh, yuck, they were just . . . you know, kind of leaning toward each other. . . . Yeesh! I can't believe I'm actually talking about my mother like this. Anyway, I could only really see her face, and it wasn't, like, all dreamy or anything. It was more . . . I don't know. Like maybe she was upset about something, and . . . I don't know."

"So we've gone from kissing, to one possible, alleged kiss," I said. "Miranda, that makes a huge difference. Why didn't you tell me all this yesterday?"

"Because there's nothing to tell," she said. "Because I really don't know anything. I thought they were kissing. Or about to kiss. But something definitely happened."

"Well can't you ask her or something?" I said.

"Are you out of your mind? Ask my mother, who I'm basically barely speaking to, if she happened to be making out with your dad last night?"

"I don't know. You seem like you're on better terms, kind of. Today."

"I guess. I mean, I wasn't expecting her to let me go with Dad, so that was sort of cool. I don't really know. I'm just really tired of fighting."

"Yeah," I said.

"So do you think there actually are bathrooms in this place?" she asked.

"Let's check it out," I said.

And eventually we found our bathrooms, and got our food, and life went on. I felt better, actually, after what Miranda said. I liked the uncertainty of it, the possibility that it was a mistake. Or something else. Wishing my father wouldn't be alone anymore was kind of different than actually dealing with the reality. Of another woman. Of Mrs. Dunham, or anybody. My father was mine, and all that I had, really. And what I really wanted, what I would have wished for if I could have had anything in the world, was for him to have my mother back. But she was gone, and she wasn't coming back. And that was just about the only thing I was completely sure about.

22

I was sitting at the kitchen table, reading the article about Llywelyn that Mrs. Dunham had lent me. She was right. It was right out of a story-book. The article talked a lot about Llywelyn's younger brother, Dafydd, the one who had started the final rebellion in which Llywelyn was killed. It said that Dafydd, who was supposedly very charming, had betrayed Llywelyn three times. First, as a young man, he had joined with their two brothers in an attempt to overthrow Llywelyn. They failed, and Dafydd was eventually forgiven. The other brothers did not get off so easily. Years later, Dafydd organized a plot to assassinate Llywelyn, but it failed. Again, Llywelyn let him live. The last betrayal was the worst. Dafydd deserted the Welsh, and joined forces with King Edward in England. I thought of Llywelyn's sad, lined face, and tried to imagine how he could press on despite such betrayal. The article seemed to suggest that Llywelyn could never find it in his heart to totally write Dafydd off. And eventually, Dafydd did come back to the Welsh, betraying the English king, to stand beside his brother in the final rebellion. It's amazing, really, the things you can forgive when you love someone. Thinking of Llywelyn and his brother, and Miranda and her father, it occurred to me that it is easier to keep loving someone, and trusting them, and taking them back, no matter what they do. Otherwise, what do you have left?

I heard my father whistling as he walked into the kitchen. Though it was still pretty early in the afternoon, the room was almost dark, as the sky had turned a deep, ominous black.

"Well, hello there," he said, giving me a big smile.

"Hi," I said, putting down the article.

"That was nice, yesterday, don't you think? At the Ty Gwyn?"

"Sure," I said.

"Things seem a little better with Miranda."

"Yeah, thank God," I laughed. "I'm starting to feel like I should be on the therapist payroll, or something."

"Cris," said my father, putting an arm around me, "you've been really wonderful. I know this isn't what you expected, getting thrust into the middle of a family feud. You're the best thing that could have happened to Miranda and Dennis. You've really made me proud of you. In your own, gentle way, you're defusing the whole situation."

"I haven't exactly been smiles and sunshine with Miranda this whole time, Dad. I tried, but I couldn't always control my temper."

"But you did it enough," he said. "Things are changing."

"I'm not really doing anything, Dad," I said, but he shook his head.

"No, you are. It's the way that you are, honey. Kind, and patient, and fair. You remind me —" His voice trailed off.

"What?" I said quickly.

"I was just going to say that you remind me of your mother."

"I do?"

"You do," he said, brushing my hair out of my eyes and staring at me for a moment.

"Anyway," he continued, taking his glasses off and rubbing his forehead, "big things in the works, so it seems."

"What do you mean?" I asked.

"Don't you guys listen to the radio? Apparently, the mother of all storms is heading this way, and we're going to be right in the middle of it."

Life's little ironies are very irritating sometimes.

"What should we do?" I asked, opening the refrigerator and staring into it, as if some answer was contained inside.

"Nothing much we can do, except hunker down and wait for it. We've got some candles in here, and I thought we might get them out in case we lose the electricity. Pretty romantic, huh?"

"You could say that," I said, closing the refrigerator door. "I should probably find Dennis, then. I know he acts like he's Superman, but the storm might throw him."

"You know, he really adores you. I'm glad he has somebody here. Before the divorce, Dennis apparently idolized his sister. They were inseparable. Things just haven't been the same between them, and I think it's been pretty hard on the little guy."

"It's no chore, Dad. I like him. I really do."

"Good. I'm glad you like Dennis. And Miranda. And . . . I mean, do you like Erica?"

"Of course," I said, examining the floor. "Why wouldn't I?"

"Good. Well. Okay."

My father has never spoken one-word sentences in his life. Maybe there was more than one storm brewing in Wales.

"Miranda, the world is about to end. The house could be consumed by lightning and reduced to a pile of rubble, and you're obsessing over house-keeping," I said, watching her make and remake her bed for the second time.

"Well, when they clear the rubble away," she said, fluffing her pillow violently, "I want them to know that one of us was neat. What do you suppose," she said, straightening, "that sheep do in a storm? Do you think they even notice?"

"Come on, let's go see Dennis," I said. "We're supposed to make sure his windows are shut."

"Why?" she asked, punching her pillow and tossing it back onto the bed.

"Let's just do. Come on. He needs you, Miranda."

"I'm the last person he needs," she said.

"I think you're the first on his list, actually. Come on. He hasn't pulled a trick in weeks, remember?"

"I had noticed that," she said. "Okay."

Dennis didn't answer when I knocked, but I opened the door, and we walked into his room. He was curled up in a little chair in front of his window, a comic book folded into his lap. He looked up as we walked in, looked past me to his sister. He looked so eager my heart leaped a little.

"Hey, squirt," she said, and he smiled.

"Hi," he said.

"My dad said there's a really big storm coming," I said, crossing to his bed and sitting down on it.

"I know," said Dennis. "I've been watching."

"We might lose electricity and everything," I said, and Dennis's face brightened.

"Are your windows shut tightly?" I asked, getting up to check them.

"Remember the big storm, Randy?" asked Dennis. "In the spring? And we got all the candles and put them all over the house?"

"And you put the candles too close to the sideboard, and they burned little black marks into the wood? I didn't know you remembered that," Miranda said, laughing.

"Mom was mad," Dennis said seriously.

"It was incredible, though. A big tree came down on our road, Cris, and took out the phone and power lines, so we had no electricity and no phones for two days. Two days! Dad made this big fire in the living room fireplace, and we all sat around it while he told ghost stories, which Mom hated because she thought Dennis would have nightmares —"

"I wasn't scared," interrupted Dennis.

"Which he totally did," Miranda continued, "for, like, days."

"Not," Dennis objected softly.

"It was great, though," she said. "It was like *Little House on the Prairie*, or something. We were totally cut off from the world."

"I remember," said Dennis.

"You know, Den," Miranda said to her brother, "you should have come to lunch with Daddy and me. He was really sad you weren't there."

"I don't want to talk to Daddy," he said.

"Why not? I know he didn't call for a couple of months, Den, but he's here now. You should spend time with him."

"I don't want to," he repeated.

"I just don't understand," said Miranda.

"I know," he said.

"And you really hurt Dad's feelings when you gave him back that present," said Miranda.

Dennis didn't say anything.

"You shouldn't have done it," she continued.

"If I take it, will you not be mad at me anymore?" he said suddenly.

That took Miranda by surprise.

"I'm not mad at you, Denny," she said.

"Are too."

She went to him, then, and put her arms around him.

"Are not."

"Are too."

"Are not. Infinity. So shut up."

He looked up at her with the same devotion Carwen had shown her father.

"Are not," he repeated.

"That's right," Miranda said, and she looked at me for a moment.

"The thing is, Den, he's coming back in a couple of days."

"I know," he said.

"And we were talking, at lunch, and I'm thinking about going with him."

"Where?" I asked.

"London. He asked if I wanted to stay with him for a while, and I do. I'm going to go with him. I think he needs me."

"No!" cried Dennis.

"I have to, Dennis," she said, and he pulled away from her.

"You said you weren't mad at me anymore!"

"I'm not! Dennis, this isn't about you. I want to go with him, Denny. He's all alone. He has no family anymore."

"No," he whimpered.

"Miranda, this is wrong," I said.

"Cris, you don't know anything about it."

"I do. You can't do this."

"It's done, Cristyn. I'm going."

My father always says there's a time to keep quiet, and there's a time to speak up. Somehow, I felt this was the time to speak up.

"Miranda, there's something you don't know about your dad."

"What are you talking about?" she said, standing.

"After he and your mom got divorced, he took Dennis. You were at a friend's house, and he went to this Little League game to see Dennis. After the game, he took him. He got like forty miles away, and then he . . ."

"What?"

"He realized it was a bad idea. He left Dennis in a gas station, and he drove away."

I looked over at Dennis, but he just stared at the floor, rolling and unrolling his comic book.

"Sick joke, Cris," said Miranda, watching her brother.

"He really wanted him, Miranda. I'm sure of that. He really wanted to be with his son, but he realized it was wrong. That Dennis belonged with his mother, and with you. It was wrong for Dennis, and it's wrong for you. You belong with your family."

"My father is my family! You're making up a story!"

"Dennis?" I said softly.

"I went to the bathroom, and he drove away," said Dennis. "Please don't be mad at me, Randy. I didn't mean to make him leave."

I was expecting Miranda to storm out of the room, as usual, but she didn't. She just sat there, staring at her brother.

"Maybe you misunderstood, Den," she said after

a while. "Maybe you were confused. You were only seven, then, right? Not eight, like you are now. Maybe you just didn't understand."

"Okay," said Dennis, whatever that meant.

I had a feeling, though, that Miranda knew the story was true. I couldn't be sure of it, but something about her expression, something in the way she was looking at her little brother, made me think she knew the truth.

"I'm supposed to check the rest of the windows," she said suddenly. "I'll be back in a minute."

This was a Miranda I'd never seen before. A Miranda who actually walked out of a room to cry.

"I'm sorry, Den," I said. "I know that was your secret, but I thought it might help to tell. Sometimes it does."

Whatever Dennis was about to say was eclipsed by an incredible clap of thunder, and suddenly it sounded as if the whole world were collapsing down onto the house.

23

My dad had ordered us all to report to the kitchen to discuss the plan of events in case "something" should happen. It's just his way, really. Miranda seemed to be pretending that nothing unusual had occurred between the three of us. She watched her brother for a moment, then turned to my father expectantly.

"First of all," my father said, after we were all seated at the kitchen table, "no one is to go outside for any reason. Okay? The winds have really picked up, and it's possible some trees could come down. And the lightning —"

"Dad," I said, "give us a little credit here. I think the last thing any of us wants to do is go out in this weather."

"Sorry," he said, a little sheepishly. "Okay, now we have enough candles here to put a few in each of your rooms. They're to be used only if the power goes out, not otherwise. We don't want to have to explain any accidents to the real estate agency. We only have one flashlight, so —"

"Two," said Dennis.

"Two?" asked my father.

"I have another one," Dennis replied.

"It's mine, Den," said Miranda.

"*We* have another one," Dennis corrected himself.

"Good. Then Dennis, if the power goes out, you're in charge of the flashlight detail."

"Okay," said Dennis, looking pleased.

"Now what else did I want to bring up?" said my father.

"Windows," said Mrs. Dunham.

"Windows, right," said my father. "Did everyone check the rooms they were supposed to? Everything tightly closed up?"

We all nodded.

"Okay, then," he said. "Just keep your eyes open. The real estate lady said that it is possible for some water to get in during a really heavy rain. I think this qualifies."

And how. The rain had been falling steadily for almost two hours, and it was growing heavier every minute. The sound of it pounding down onto the slate roof was almost deafening. It was like being at the foot of an enormous waterfall. The thunder and lighting were happening much closer together now, which I knew meant that the storm was coming closer.

"Anything else?" my dad asked. "Erica?"

She shook her head. "We'll be working in the study, as usual, if any of you need us."

"All right, then," said my father, getting to his feet. Mrs. Dunham got up, too, and stood beside him.

"I just —" Mrs. Dunham began, "that is — I would feel a lot better if the three of you stuck together. I know you'll all be inside, but I just worry about losing the lights. Do you think —"

"No problem," I said.

"We'll stay together," Miranda added, watching her brother.

"I'll take care of them, Mom," said Dennis, and I think we all actually smiled at that.

No one said anything else as Dad and Mrs. Dunham walked out of the room, back to that place where they spent so much time together.

"Does it ever stop raining in this country?" asked Miranda. "What are we going do all night?"

"We could play Scrabble," I suggested, but Miranda, making a slight gesture toward her brother, shook her head no.

"Monopoly?" I said.

"Blech," said Dennis, jumping slightly as another crack of thunder erupted.

"What, then?" I asked.

"I want to go to the cellar," said Miranda.

"Now?" I asked. "In this?"

"Why not? We said we wouldn't go outside. We didn't say anything about the cellar. Anyway, what difference does it make?"

It made all the difference, I thought, because the next time I see Carwen may be the last.

"Okay," said Dennis suddenly.

"Really?" said Miranda. "Cris?"

I sighed and ran my hands through my hair.

"I guess now is as good a time as any," I said, and Miranda jumped up.

"Great!"

"Should we tell them where we're going?" I asked.

"I'm not going in there," Miranda said. "Come on, Den. Got the light?"

Dennis nodded, producing the flashlight.

"Then let's go," she said, and we did.

The sounds of the storm were still evident as we walked down the stairs, but they were muffled, as if someone had put a giant pillow over the roof. Dennis went first, lighting the way, and Miranda clung to my arm as we descended the steps. Dennis uttered a little cry as he reached the bottom.

"What's wrong?" I asked, watching him shine the light onto the floor. It seemed to be moving. "What is it?"

"Water," he said. "Almost up to my ankles."

"Where is it coming from?" asked Miranda.

"I don't know," he replied.

"We should go back up and tell them," I said.

"No way!" said Miranda. "There's nothing down here to ruin, right? Besides, what are they going to do about it tonight?"

"Not much, I guess," I said, and Miranda pulled me down to the bottom with her.

"Come on," she said. "I hate these shoes anyway."

The water was freezing, and I shivered as it seeped into my sneakers and socks.

"Where is she?" asked Miranda, and Dennis pointed the way to the hollow under the stairs with his flashlight.

"Where?" Miranda repeated.

There was nothing there. Nothing but smooth, dark wall glimmering wetly.

"Just wait for a little while," I said uncertainly. A little while passed.

"Cristyn . . ." said Miranda.

"I don't know!" I said. "She usually just . . . she usually —"

"You're tooling on me!" she cried. "I can't believe I fell for this! I can't believe I'm standing in ice water up to my ankles waiting for Casper the

Friendly Medieval Ghost to drop by! I'm out of here!"

She turned abruptly and began wading to the stairs. I lunged for her, grabbing her shirt in one hand, and I succeeded in holding her there for a moment.

"Damn it, Cristyn!" she yelled. "Let me —"

The sound was earsplitting, as if the entire house had been split down the middle. I shrieked and jumped forward, and, losing my sense of balance in the darkness, I fell heavily into the cold water, dragging Miranda down with me. She fell partially on top of me, pushing my face into the icy wetness. Struggling, I pulled free of her and threw my head back, spitting out dirt and water and gasping for breath. Just as I began to get my bearings back, I became aware of the orange glow that had flooded the basement, and the sound of a fire crackling dangerously close by.

"It's on fire!" cried Miranda, dragging me to my feet. "Dennis! Come on, we've got to get out of here!"

"No, wait! It's Carwen, Miranda. Look! Look!"

She turned toward the source of the glow, her eyes wide.

"It's a fire, Cris!"

"It's her fire. A ghost fire. Watch."

I could see a figure, through the smoke, and the sounds became clearer, the roaring of the fire and something else. Other voices, men's voices, shouting above the flames.

"Oh, my God," murmured Miranda. "Then it's really true."

Carwen held a bag in one hand and was frantically filling it with something. Her face was darkened with smoke, and as she coughed and struggled something heavy fell beside her, a thick timber covered with flames. From somewhere, I heard the sound of a horse whinnying in fear.

"Carwen, go!" I shouted. "Get out!"

She had dropped the bag when the timber fell and was on her hands and knees retrieving its contents. She started to get up, but another piece of burning wood fell, hitting her on the shoulder, and she dropped back to the ground.

I tried to move toward her, but Miranda was clutching me so tightly I couldn't move. I caught a quick glimpse of Dennis's face, drawn and anxious in the strange light.

Carwen climbed unsteadily back to her feet and began to move toward her door, but she stopped, suddenly, her hand flying up to her throat. She began to look wildly around the floor as the smoke grew steadily thicker.

"What is it?" said Miranda. "Why doesn't she leave?"

She got back on her hands and knees, running her hands frantically over the floor.

"Her pendant," I whispered. "Her necklace. Her father gave her a necklace the last time he saw her."

Carwen knelt, weeping, on the ground, and I heard the sound of men's voices again, angry, and closing in.

"Run!" I screamed, and her head jerked up and she looked straight into my eyes.

Suddenly, she was on her feet running toward me, and the scene blinked off, the orange glow suddenly gone. But something was wrong. The cellar was dark and the fire gone, but the smell was still thick in the air. Dennis shined his light up toward the steps, and we could all see that the smoke billowing in under the door was no phantom projection. This fire was real.

24

We moved quickly up the stairs and through the oak door, but the smoke was much thicker on the small landing, and when I touched the door to the kitchen, it was hot. I thought I heard the sound of my father's voice, calling my name.

"We're here!" I screamed.

"Don't come through," he cried. "Get away from the door, and keep low!"

"What?" cried Miranda. "What is he saying?"

"Come on," I said, pulling her back with me. "We've got to get down lower. The smoke will rise."

The three of us moved like one person, our arms wrapped around each other. We went back through the oak door and shut it behind us.

"We'll be okay here," I said, pulling them down

close to me on the steps. "Don't panic. Is every-body okay?"

"Dennis?" asked Miranda, putting her arms around her weeping brother. "How're you doing?"

"Don't go, Randy," he whimpered, burying his face in her arms.

"We're all going to stay together, Den," I said. "Don't worry. My dad is taking care of everything."

"Don't go, Randy," he repeated, and she rocked him gently back and forth, smoothing his hair. Though I was glad, truly glad, to see Miranda comforting her brother, I was surprised at the little flame of jealousy that flared up in me as he clung to her.

"What's happening up there?" asked Miranda.

"I don't know," I said. "Something must have gone up in flames in the kitchen."

"Do you think they're okay?" she asked.

"I heard my father's voice," I said. "I'm sure they're fine. And we're safe down here. There's like an entire lake on the floor. We'll be fine."

"I saw her, Cris," Miranda whispered.

"I know."

"I really saw her," she repeated.

Suddenly I heard my father's voice again. "Cris? Where are you?" he called.

"Dad!" I cried, jumping to my feet, as the oak

door above us opened, and his anxious face peered through.

"Are you all here? Is everyone okay? Come on, quickly. The fire's out, but we need to get out of the area."

We scrambled back up the stairs and through the kitchen, a blurry mess of smoke and glass I barely noticed as he led us into the study. Mrs. Dunham rushed to her children and put her arms around them.

"What happened?" I said to my father, who was looking at me as if I'd come back from the dead.

"Are you all right?" he said, so softly I almost couldn't hear him.

"I'm fine, Dad. What happened?"

"I'm not sure. I think lightning must have hit the tree outside the kitchen, and a big section of it crashed through the kitchen window and knocked over the wood-burning stove. The curtains caught on fire, and then the table . . . we couldn't find you!"

"We were in the cellar," I said, as if that would explain everything.

"We couldn't find you," he repeated, touching my face with his hand. He was shaking. Really, seriously shaking.

"We kept calling, we kept — oh, Gwen . . ."

That was the first time in my life, ever, that my father called me by my mother's name.

We cleaned up as much of the mess as we could that night. The limb of the tree stuck strangely through the window, and water dripped steadily through onto the floor. We left the wood-burning stove lying partially on its side, like a fallen hero.

"What a disaster area," I said, sweeping up the last of the glass. "Are we going to get in trouble?"

"I think this falls under the category of an act of God," my father said, still looking shaken.

"What's an act of God?" asked Dennis, squirming under his mother's grasp.

"Not our fault," I said, and my father smiled a little.

"But why did you go into the cellar? How did you get so wet?" asked Mrs. Dunham, taking her daughter's hand in her own. Miranda didn't pull away, I noticed.

"Lucky we did," I said, examining the remains of the kitchen table. "That's where we were sitting just before we left."

"Don't even say it," said Mrs. Dunham, raising Miranda's hand and pressing it against her face. "Thank you for staying with him, sweetheart. Thank you for taking care of yourselves."

Miranda didn't say anything, but she left her hand against her mother's cheek for a moment.

"I don't think there is much more we can do here tonight," said my father. "Enough is enough. Let's all try to get some sleep, and we'll deal with this in the morning."

"Okay," I said, as my father put his arms around me. It was a good feeling, having him so close, comfortable and familiar. Safe.

"Do you want to sleep with us tonight, Den?" asked Miranda. "Cris?"

"Sure, no problem," I said, but Dennis shook his head.

"Oh, come on, squirt," she said. "What if we need you?"

He gave the matter some serious thought, then said, "Call for me. I'll come right away."

I had my last dream about Carwen that night, and the scene played itself out to the end. She ran for her horse, struggling as the animal reared in fear from the fire. She climbed onto him and tried desperately to control him. For a minute the horse was calm, and in that moment she brought her hand again to her throat, searching for her father's necklace, leaving only one hand loosely gripping the reins. It was then that the horse bolted, and she may never fully have regained her balance. I went with her this time, as the horse galloped furiously away from the burning cottage, down into the woods where the light again grew dim. I was with her as she careened through the trees, dangerously off balance and clinging to the horse's mane, and I was with her when the horse veered suddenly to the left, throwing her long and hard onto the ground, where she lay, unmoving and silent.

25

In addition to the wreckage in the kitchen, we had discovered that by the time the rain finally stopped, almost a half foot of water had flooded the basement. My father made some calls and found a man who was willing to come with a generator-operated pump to take the water out. He also brought a chain saw, and together with his son, they reduced the once mighty limb to a neat pile of firewood, which they stacked in the backyard.

In what had to be an apology for its previously bad behavior, the weather was spectacular. There wasn't a cloud to be seen for miles, and the sun beat down on the soaking landscape.

Miranda and Dennis and I worked tirelessly in the kitchen cleaning the remains of the mess. The room, once so cozy, looked sad and battle-worn, the black marks from the fire scarring the old stone walls.

Dennis helped me carry some of the water-soaked remains of the curtains outside. I left him there, marveling over the burned fabric, and went back into the kitchen for the rest of it. Mrs. Dunham was there, and Miranda was speaking to her quietly. They didn't seem to notice I was there, or if they did, they didn't seem to care.

"I know about it all, now, Mom," Miranda was saying. "I know what he did with Dennis. I know why he didn't call for so long."

"How?"

"Dennis knows. He's always known."

"I didn't want you to have to know that, either of you," Mrs. Dunham said softly. "I'm so sorry, honey."

"Why didn't you tell me?" Miranda asked.

"I didn't want you to think I was trying to turn you against him. I want you to have a relationship with him, sweetheart. You deserve that. You deserve a lot more. It was so stupid of me to think Dennis didn't know what actually happened."

"If you had told me, though, I might have understood. I could have been so much nicer . . ."

"Would it have really made a difference?" Mrs. Dunham asked. Miranda hesitated, then shook her head.

"Maybe not. Maybe. I don't know. But it makes

a difference now, Mom. I'm really sorry I was such a brat."

I grabbed the rest of the curtain and walked quickly out of the room, but not before I saw Miranda put her arms around her mother and hug. Tightly.

When Mrs. Dunham pronounced the cleanup detail officially over, all five of us went out back and sat outside, enjoying the sunshine.

"I spoke to the real-estate lady," said my father, sipping a glass of soda. "We're in the clear. All damages covered."

"Thank heaven for that," said Mrs. Dunham, giving him a smile.

We heard footsteps, and a craggy-faced man in muddy overalls and tall, wet Wellington boots rounded the back of the house.

"Mr. Stone?" he said, and my father got to his feet.

"How's it going down there?" he asked.

"We've got all the water out. It will just be another few minutes or so, to pack up our gear," the man said, speaking in a wonderful Welsh lilt.

"Fantastic," said my father. "Thank you, Mr. Jones."

"We found something down there," he said, extending his hand. "Looks like a necklace. Our pumping must have brought it to the top of the mud."

"Really?" said my father. "Let's have a look."

Mr. Jones held it up for us to see as I leaned forward eagerly.

"Hard to tell what it is, exactly," he said, "all covered with mud the way it is. Could be quite old, or could be something the last tenant left behind. I've got a friend in town, works for the Historical Society. I can have him take a look at it, if you don't mind."

"That would be wonderful," said Mrs. Dunham. "Would you let us know if you find out it's old?"

"That I will," he said. "I'll just pick it up from you on my way out, if you'd like to have a look at it now."

"Thanks," my dad said. "I appreciate it."

Mr. Jones gave a nod and walked back down the path.

"Can I see it?" Dennis said quickly, before I had a chance to say anything. "Please?"

"Sure," said my father. "Just be careful with it. If it is a period piece, it might be very fragile."

Dennis took the necklace carefully and climbed out of his chair.

"There's a magnifying glass in the study," he said. "I'm going to get it!"

He dashed into the house before anyone could stop him.

"Denny, be careful with it!" his mother called after him.

"Looks like everyone's developing an interest in history these days," said my father, smiling. "I hope he's not disappointed. It's probably nothing."

"Probably," I said, a little too loudly, and Miranda nodded.

"I just can't get over that kitchen," said Mrs. Dunham. "Whatever possessed you all to go into the cellar? I didn't want to say anything in front of Dennis, but you could have been seriously hurt if you'd stayed in the kitchen, between the fire and the flying glass. What made you go down there? Did you think it would be safer?"

"Much as I would love to take credit, Mom, we weren't thinking about safety. We were bored. We just wanted to explore."

"Thank God for that," said my father, shaking his head and giving me a long look. "Finally something good came of the fact that you guys have nothing to do around here. Erica and I are going to do some serious planning, guys. We're going to make sure you three don't have to sit around playing in the cellar for the rest of the summer."

"What are we going to do about the window?" Miranda asked. "And the stove?"

"Well, the stove looks fine, actually," said my father. "It looks to me like it just got knocked forward hard enough for some of the embers to fly out. I should have realized it was too close to those curtains, though. And the real-estate lady gave me a number to call to get the glass replaced. Won't be today though, so I guess it will be a little chilly in there tonight."

"Tonight?" I asked. "When isn't it chilly in that house?"

Dennis rounded the corner of the house quickly, like a man with a mission.

"Hi," he said and handed the necklace back to my father. "It's too dirty," he said. "I can't see anything. I was afraid to wash it."

"Good thinking," said my father.

"So, Dad, how long do you think it will be before we get the necklace back?" I asked.

"Well, if it turns out to be really old, I guess we won't get it back," he replied.

"What? But it's ours!"

"No, it isn't, honey. We don't own this house. Plus, if it really is an artifact, it belongs in a museum."

"But they found it because of us! We didn't have to say anything about it! He has to bring it back!"

"It's not ours to keep, Cris. I'm sorry."

"You can't give it to him, Dad!"

"Cris, I have to. Come on, now. You know we can't keep something like that. It wouldn't be right!"

I had messed everything up. I hadn't been quick enough, hadn't been thinking fast, and now it was too late. I knew now what Carwen wanted, why she'd lingered in the house for so long. The necklace her father had given her was the most precious thing she had. It was the last thing he'd given her, maybe the only thing he'd given her, to remember him by. And she wanted it back. She'd wanted me to get it back for her. And now it was going to end up in a museum, lost to Carwen forever. If I had more time, maybe I could think of something, but there was no time, because Mr. Jones was coming back down the path, and my father was handing the necklace to him.

"Let us know what you find out," my father said. "My daughter is particularly interested in this piece."

"I will," said Mr. Jones, wrapping Carwen's necklace in a handkerchief. "Tell you what, young lady, if it turns out to be new, I'll bring it back for you to wear."

"Thanks," I said, turning my face away.

"Thank you, sir," my father said, and Mr. Jones gave a nod, pocketed Carwen's necklace, and left.

I was a complete and utter failure.

"I guess I'll go have a look down in the cellar," my father said. "Want to come?"

"Actually, Dad, that's, like, the last place I want to see right now."

"Okay."

"Well, I would like to see this famous cellar," said Mrs. Dunham, getting to her feet. "I feel like I owe it a debt of gratitude, or something."

"Maybe you could wallpaper it," said my father, grinning. Then he turned to look at us.

"Hey," he said. "You all were great today. We couldn't have gotten that mess cleaned up without you. And I was serious about making plans for stuff for you all to do. We'll start first thing tomorrow. A day trip, or something. Whatever you guys want."

"Thanks, Mr. Stone," said Miranda.

"Thank you," said my father, strolling off with Mrs. Dunham to explore the muddy shambles that had once been Carwen's home. As soon as he was out of sight, I covered my face with my hands and groaned.

"What's wrong?" asked Miranda.

"What's wrong?" I repeated. "Did you not just witness the same thing that I witnessed?"

"What are you talking about?" Miranda asked.

"Don't be mad, Randy, okay?" asked Dennis.

"I'm not mad, Den. Cristyn, what?"

"Really, don't be mad," said Dennis again.

"The necklace!" I cried.

"The necklace Carwen lost?" Miranda said.

"Promise?" asked Dennis. "Cross your heart you won't be mad?"

"Squirt, I'm not mad at you. You mean you think that's what that guy found down there?"

"That's what she wanted, Miranda! That's what this whole thing was about! If I'd been thinking, if I'd been paying attention I could have figured out that it was still down there. That's what she was trying to show us! That she lost the necklace down there, in our cellar. She brought us down there because the flood was bringing it up to the surface. We were supposed to get it back! And now that man's taken it, and Carwen's never going to get it back!"

"He didn't take it," said Dennis.

"He did take it, Den!" I said, frustrated. "He put it in his pocket and walked away."

"That was Miranda's necklace," said Dennis.

"No, Den, my necklace is upstairs by my bed."

"Not anymore," said Dennis. "I switched them. I took your necklace, Randy, and I rubbed mud into it, and I gave it to the man. Are you mad?"

"Are you serious?" she asked. Dennis reached

into his pocket and pulled out a little bundle. Opening it carefully, he showed me the muddy little treasure nestled inside.

"Dennis," I shrieked, throwing my arms around him, "you are an angel!"

26

In the morning, as Dad and Mrs. Dunham were doing the breakfast dishes, we cleaned off the necklace as best we could, gently, then sat on the floor in my room, making a small circle around it.

"So you're saying she died that night?" Miranda asked, and I nodded.

"That's so sad," she said.

"In a way," I said. "But what did she have left in Dolwyddelan? Her father and her stepmother were dead, probably everyone her father knew was dead or in prison. How could she have survived, alone like that? At least she can be with her father now. When we give her back her necklace."

"Give it back how?" asked Dennis.

"Yeah, we don't even know where her . . . we don't even know where she is now," said Miranda.

"I'm not sure," I said. "But I think I know a way. I'd like to . . . do it alone. Would that be okay?"

"What way?" said Miranda. Dennis folded the necklace back into the handkerchief and handed it to me.

"Okay, Cristyn," said Dennis.

"Okay?" said Miranda. "What's so important that you can't do it with us?"

"She wanted Cristyn," said Dennis. "From the beginning. She wanted Cristyn."

"Thanks a lot," said Miranda.

"No," I said, "I couldn't have done it at all without you guys. Really. But I just — I can't explain it. I just feel like I need to do this by myself. Please?"

"Okay," said Dennis again, and Miranda reluctantly nodded.

"But you'll tell us about it? Right?" she said.

"I'll tell you everything," I said, putting the wrapped necklace into my pocket.

The grass was still wet as I walked down the lawn, over the stone bridge, and onto the path into the woods, the path over which Carwen had ridden so many years ago. It had only been a hunch, but when I came into the stone circle, I knew without a doubt that Carwen was buried there. Whether the rocks had been set up around her grave, or whether they'd been there much longer I'd never know, nor would I know who had buried her. But she was resting there, in the center of the rocks. I was certain.

I went straight to the center of the circle and

pulled away the wet earth. It came away easily in my hands, and I had no trouble in making quite a good hole. When I was satisfied that it was deep enough, I took the necklace from my pocket.

"Here it is, Carwen," I said, placing it into the hole. "I've brought it back."

I carefully refilled the hole and packed the dirt down firmly on top of it. Then I chose the smallest of the stones in the circle, pried it loose, and wedged it tightly on top of the hole. I was sitting back to admire my work when I felt her presence, very strongly. I turned and looked straight into her face. And this time, it was like she was really there.

"Carwen," I whispered, and she heard me and broke into a beautiful smile.

"Thank you," she said, her accent thick and strange.

"I can understand you!" I said, and she smiled again.

"I'm so sorry," I said, my voice trembling, "about Llywelyn, about everything."

"No," she said, "I can join my father now. You have broken the circle."

I thought she might be about to blink out right then and there, so I spoke quickly.

"I don't — Carwen, if you could talk to me, like you are now, why didn't you just ask me? In the beginning?"

She looked lost in thought for a moment, and then she spoke.

"I could not. The . . . things that you saw happening to me, those moments, were like a circle. They held me inside them. I became the circle, and I moved around it, living the moments again and again, until I almost forgot that there had ever been anything else. I became a prisoner. And after a long time, I stopped trying to get out. I stopped trying to do anything. I remembered nothing else. The circle was the only living left to me. And then, one day, a girl came. And it was as if I began to awaken."

"Because of me?" I asked.

"Because of both of you," she said.

"Both of us?" I asked, but she continued.

"She would come down into the cellar and sit. As if she knew I was there. As if she were waiting. It took a long time for me to understand, and when I did, I found I did not know how to speak to her. And then, one day, she was gone, and I fell back into my dream. And I waited for her to return. I do not know how long I waited, but one day I found she had returned. She was older, but her face looked the same."

"I had been asleep, in a way, dreaming that circle, for so long, I did not know I could do anything else. I did not know how to speak, did not know if

I could. It was as if I had to learn to walk, to move, to think, all over again. I found I could move things, and that became my way of speaking. She did not come down and sit with me as she had done before. I tried to bring her back down, under the stairs, to me, and one day she came, and I found I had been wrong. It was a different girl. It was you. I am afraid I may have frightened you. I had to learn, each time, the things that would reach you, and the things that would frighten you away."

I thought of the oak door slamming and the sound of the dead bolt sliding closed. It seemed almost comical now. If only I had known.

"But didn't you come to me in this stone circle? That time?"

"Here?" she said, looking around. "No. I have not been here since . . . I do not remember when. Lifetimes."

Who then? Who had been with me in the circle that day?

"It was so difficult," she continued, "to reach you. Though the child seemed to understand."

"Dennis?" I asked.

"Dennis," she said thoughtfully. "And he finally brought you to me."

"When I saw my father for the last time, he gave me the necklace," she continued. "He had given it once before, to my mother, and he carried it with him after she died. He told me the necklace was blessed and represented the bond between us. As long as I carried it with me, he said, part of him would be with me, too. No matter where he was. No matter what happened to either of us. When I lost the necklace, I lost him. And now I have him back. You did that."

"Why, Carwen? What exactly was it that woke you up after all that time?"

"The girl, because she was so like me, as I was once. Because she was listening. And you, because you were just like her. I only realized you were not the same girl when you came down into the cellar, and I saw your hair. Not red, like hers. But for that, you could have been one and the same."

"Red hair," I murmured, feeling my face grow pale.

"Now that I see you both together, I understand."

"You see us both?" I asked softly. "Now? You see us both?" She nodded.

"I thank you," she said. "I thank you both. For my father. He is waiting for me."

Whether she blinked out, faded away, or simply walked out of the picture I'll never know, because my eyes were so full of tears I could see nothing at all. I wasn't crying because Carwen had left, though. I was crying because although she had gone, I was still not alone in the circle. My mother was there, too. She'd been with me all along.

I was still crying when I walked into the study. Mrs. Dunham took one look at my face, grabbed a book, and beat a hasty retreat, closing the door behind her. My father came to me quickly and took me in his arms.

"Baby, what is it?" he asked. "What's wrong?"

"I want to know about her!" I sobbed. "Daddy, I want to know."

"About who, sweetheart?"

"My mother," I wept.

"Oh, Cristyn," he said softly, running a hand through my hair. "Of course you do. I'm so sorry, baby. I'm so terribly sorry."

"Why don't we ever talk about her?" I asked, sorry for the sadness I saw creep into his face, but needing to know even more.

"I don't know, sweetheart. I just don't know. For a long, long time, I couldn't even think about her. It was all so fresh, and so painful, and I just couldn't. And then, after a while, it hurt less, but it never really went away. I wanted to tell you about her so many times, but I just couldn't get started. I didn't know how to talk about her. I didn't know what you wanted. And you didn't ask, but why should you? You shouldn't have had to ask."

"I didn't want to upset you," I said. "I thought I was too little when she died — that I didn't remember her well enough to miss her. But I do, Daddy! I miss her so much."

"I know you do, Cris. I know you do."

"Will you tell me about her?"

He looked into my eyes for a long moment and nodded.

"She was beautiful, like you are, but her hair was this wild red color, so lovely. Gwynedd was her home, where she was born. Her parents brought her to the States when she was ten. She could speak Welsh, did you know that? It was such an incredible thing to hear, those rolling r's and those impossible words. She used to sing you these little Welsh lullabies; God, you loved them so much. She had a beautiful voice, and you used to beg her to sing those songs again and again. Especially the one about Llywelyn. That was your favorite. I was so surprised when you asked about him. I hadn't thought you remembered."

"Where did you meet her?" I asked.

"She was teaching school in Maine, near where I was studying. I used to see her in this little bookstore in town; she was always there. She loved to read, just like you do. One day I asked her to come have a cup of tea with me, and we must have had ten cups between us! We talked and talked. She was so passionate about her history, so proud. I had access to all of the medieval history books at the university, and she used to pore over them for hours. I wanted you to see this country, Cris, because she loved it so much."

"Do you ever feel angry at her for leaving you all alone?"

"Sometimes I feel angry, yes. But not at her. I get mad at the world, sometimes, because she isn't in it anymore. But she didn't leave me all alone. She left me with you, sweetheart," he said.

"But you know, Dad. What I mean."

"I know," he said softly. "How would you feel, Cris, if there were someone else?"

"Glad," I said quickly, making myself believe it. "It would be weird, at first, but I'd be glad. Is it Mrs. Dunham?"

He rubbed his forehead thoughtfully and sighed.

"I don't know, Cris. Something is happening, yes. Something has happened. I don't know what it means, and I don't think she does, either. Maybe something. Maybe nothing."

"You should be with someone, Dad," I said. "The word is you're pretty cute."

"There's a word? On me?" he asked, raising an eyebrow, and I laughed.

"Tell me more about her, Dad," I said. "Tell me everything."

It took a long time, there in our old stone house in the heart of Wales, and I'm sure he didn't tell me everything, but he told me a lot. Worlds.

ELIZABETH CODY KIMMEL has loved ghost stories since she was a girl, and for many years she has been captivated by the people and events of medieval Wales. After a recent trip to Wales, including a visit to Gwynedd's Dolwyddelan Castle, she felt compelled to write this novel in order to bring the people and times closer to contemporary readers.

Elizabeth Cody Kimmel lives in New York City. *In the Stone Circle* is her first novel.